Mina Cortez: Bouquets to Bullets

By

Jeffrey Cook

F & I
by Melange Books

Published by
Fire and Ice
A Young Adult Imprint of Melange Books, LLC
White Bear Lake, MN 55110
www.fireandiceya.com

Mina Cortez: Bouquets to Bullets ~ Copyright © 2014 by Jeffrey Cook

ISBN: 978-1-68046-035-3

Cover Art by Caroline Andrus

This book is dedicated to Kaylin Anderson and Mike Decuir, without whom this book wouldn't exist. Everyone needs the type of friends who will ask the truly important questions, such as: "What if no one truly did expect the Spanish Inquisition, including the Spanish Inquisition? How would that work?" Sometimes random moments really can become whole stories.

Thank you for read and reviews, and supporting the indie community.

Jeffrey Cook

Chapter One

Mina raced down the alleyway, dodging past people on foot and around a recycling bin. As her bike hit a long stretch of open path, she crouched forward and pushed herself faster. Her pulse pounded. She couldn't slow down. Her wrist-comm chimed to tell her how late she was running. This almost distracted her from a bright light flashing up ahead of her at the edge of the alleyway where it opened up onto the street. Seeing figures moving against the movement of the light, she braked hard. Instead of stopping, the bike went into a skid in the loose gravel and pooled rainwater, then tumbled. Mina hit the ground hard, momentum carrying her skidding along the alley floor just behind her bicycle.

She came to a stop a few feet from the edge of the alleyway, her bike clattering down the dirty path. Mina saw a tall figure moving in its path. She had barely opened her mouth to shout a warning when the woman turned, lifted a foot, and stepped down with perfect timing to bring the bike to an abrupt halt.

Mina pushed up to her feet after a moment, clutching her now-sore wrist. "I'm so, so sorry," she offered, abruptly but sincerely.

The big woman, easily a head and a half taller than Mina, scowled down at her. As she closed the gap, Mina noticed an area cordoned off by the police, just a few yards back from the edge of the alley, and a number of officers scrambling around setting up tape, a couple of cars currently blocking the street—the source of the lights she'd seen earlier.

"Sorry," Mina said again.

The woman's eyes did not soften as she shifted, blocking Mina's view of the scene. "You shouldn't be here. Move," she said directly, leaving no room for question.

1

Mina quickly gathered up her bike and started away from the scene as quickly as possible. Her wrist-comm buzzed, and a voice called over it, "Incoming, get ready to go!"

Mina looked down the street to see her best friend's car careening down the road with Amiko's typically lead-footed driving style. "Miko, there's police down here!" she called back into the comm.

Vlad, Amiko's restored ancient model Chevy, screeched to a sudden slowdown, eventually pulling up at something akin to polite suburban driving speeds.

"Get in!" called the cheery voice of the Asian girl in the fedora. Mina pressed two buttons on the frame of her bike and quickly folded it up to fit neatly in the back seat of Miko's car. Then she launched herself into the passenger seat as the comforting scent of sandalwood and cloves hit her. Mina always appreciated Miko's post-tai-chi smell, but knew not to mention it. The younger girl was still a little awkward over the fact she did it alone each morning now.

"Can you see that woman with the cyber arm? I think I already got my first two warnings." Mina commented, only half joking.

"Yeah, I see her not being happy." Miko squinted. "How do you know she has a cybernetic arm?"

"Would you drive? We're going to be late!" Mina said, punching her friend in the shoulder.

Miko hit the gas, and the car launched ahead. The acceleration wasn't as smooth as any kind of modern car, and Mina was pitched forward midway through buckling herself in, since it didn't have automatically adjusting straps. "Damn it."

"So how did you know she had a cyberlimb?" came the question again. "It had to be a good one." Miko was unperturbed as usual.

"They're getting way better with the synth skin, but it's still always a shade or two off," Mina replied as she finished buckling in. A block later, just outside of standard police-scan range, Miko hit the gas again, tearing around a corner. Anything modern, outside an emergency vehicle, wouldn't have let them get over the local speed limit. But Vlad was from another time, excavated from an old parking garage that had been buried in the quakes. One of Dr. Kimura's research digs had found it in almost prime condition from the sealed environment. He and Miko, in one of their last father-daughter collaborations, had spent more than a year testing and restoring it to working order, and using his University clout to get the permits for a fuel-based hybrid vehicle without self-correction. The 2040 Impala was way before the safety-assurance regs.

"So, why aren't you in school?" Mina asked, tensing a bit as Miko raced around a corner. No matter how often she rode with her best friend, Mina never entirely got used to Miko's driving habits, especially when she was in a hurry.

"All for one," Miko teased. "I checked your GPS co-ords. You weren't going to make it."

"And now we're not going to make it," Mina muttered back.

"Oh ye of little faith." Her best friend grinned, kissed two fingers, and pressed them to her "Saint Elwood" bobblehead, another relic—and Miko's hero. "Our Lady of Blessed Acceleration, don't fail us now."

Mina rolled her eyes, and then shut them tight and clutched the handle harder as Vlad jolted up to top speed, only slowing a slight bit around corners. Thankfully, early-morning traffic around the back streets was light, and Miko kept away from main thoroughfares when speeding. "So what do you figure the big police fuss was?" she asked as she drove.

Mina's knee-jerk reaction was to tell her to watch the road, but she'd gotten mostly used to her friend's driving by now. "No idea. Plain clothes, no burning smell like with big accidents—some kind of raid, maybe. The big lady didn't want me looking, and I wasn't about to question it."

"You and your nose." Miko smirked. "If you weren't on your way to Russia for the Bolshoi Ballet, you could ask them for a police dog chip. That'd get you out of delivering flowers."

Mina slumped a bit lower in her seat. "I'm not going to Russia," she muttered.

"Are you sure? You've worked hard for it, and I don't seem to recall you having a chipping date yet. No one deserves a magical-ballerina microchip more than you," Miko shot back.

"You know I haven't. You'll be the second to know."

"I'd better be. And until you get it, I'm not going to let you give up."

"They don't need short, stocky ballerinas in Russia. In New York, either. Face it. You're stuck with me."

"The horror," Miko teased. "Seriously though, 'til you get it, you don't know for sure, right?"

Mina shook her head. "You're impossible." Despite the words, she couldn't help but smile a little. They both knew that if she'd gotten into any other ballet academy, she definitely would have heard by now to start getting ready for the move this close to chipping. While its decision date was later, the Russian academy's standards were certainly no lower—especially for international applicants—which made it the longest of long-shots. Still, being a ballerina had been Mina's goal since they were both tiny, right up until she never got that last growth spurt.

"Okay, almost to school. Get ready to run."

Mina blinked out of her brief reverie as they reached the school lot, her comm giving her the two-minute warning. The car jolted, not quite jumping the curb, but catching the edge of the turn in with one tire. Miko had to park out near the back of the lot near the staff and rec vehicles, since Vlad wouldn't fit in any of the main spots.

"Can you drop me off at the shop after dance class?" Mina asked as they were pulling in. Thankfully, there wasn't enough space for Miko to even try a fishtail parking job. She'd never quite managed one, but that didn't stop her from trying.

"Yeah, no problem. Got to run Scott home anyway so he'll be on time to watch the munchkin. We'll be going right past. Besides, this is the last time we're running him home, so you should definitely come."

"You really think he's going to be in the first wave of microchip assignments next week?" Mina asked leaving her bike in the back and jumping out as soon as they'd come to a stop.

"Sure of it," Miko called, pulling herself directly out through the car window and taking off after her towards the school as time ticked down.

"True, with his parents' clout, he's bound to either end up getting a first wave job, or assigned to the lunar colony," Mina called back as the neared the school.

"No way he's going back to the moon after all his parents did to raise a kid ... not on the moon," Miko answered.

The Szachs had, in the interest of their kids' socialization, not only transferred off the colony to Seattle, but stayed out of the child-sparse neighborhoods of their own socioeconomic bracket. Of course, in the girls' opinion, it had paid off. They'd met the Cortezes and Kimuras. Who wouldn't want to send their son trick-or-treating with five-and six-year-old Miko and Mina Mouse? Oh, sure, the parents had become good friends, too, eventually collaborating on park restoration projects—Dr. Kimura for the historical reconstruction, the Cortezes for the landscaping, the Szachs for the cash—but the kids had become the inseparable Mouseketeers.

The pair came to a stop, then moved through the front door scanners at normal speed, their comms beeping an indication they were clear through security and not so late as to need to head anywhere besides class. A good start.

"I know he requested not-Luna, but if he got something that high profile ... those are some of the top jobs going if you've got the computer brain."

"Pft, he's in the running to be a chip programmer."

"Hardly anyone gets to be a—"

Mina gestured for silence. "A chip programmer. He'll stay in Seattle for that. I've got to keep one of you, and you're going to Russia," Miko answered self-assuredly as they stepped into their first period Social Arts class.

* * * *

Body wash. Being hit by the scent as she walked into the room half-full of teenage boys was one of Mina's least favorite things, but it was better than being late again. They entered just before the first bell rang.

"Hats off in class, Miss Kimura," Mr. Phelps said, without turning from getting the lesson holo up. Miko cheerily set her black fedora on her desk before getting her keyboard and holo reader out and set up. Mina, too, opened up the display at her desk for the three-dimensional lesson presentation.

"You need to stop cutting it so close," Scott Szach whispered from his seat in the aisle next to theirs. He plugged his input wire directly into his cybernetic eye, letting him process the input and respond purely with eye movement.

"My fault," Mina conceded. "Parents kept me up doing inventory half the night again—" The horticulturists behind some of the city's biggest projects were in high demand in general, and she was their only daughter. Which also meant it was generally assumed she'd end up, like her mother before her, a shop assistant and delivery girl from the end of school until her parents' retirement. "—and wouldn't let me borrow the van." That was common enough, too. The van was an occasional perk for big deliveries. Mostly, there was the collapsible emerald-and-lilac bicycle. "Miko would have made it easy if she hadn't gone back to get me."

"Yeah, but where would the fun in that be?" Miko replied with a wink, all three shutting up when the teacher turned back around.

Mr. Phelps stepped away from the holographic display on Pacific Rim relations to address the class. "All right, I know a lot of you are in the clutches of short-timer's syndrome, especially among our seniors. First chipping wave begins next week, and a few of you may not be here tomorrow for prep." Half the class looked at Scott at that. His family already had top-level security clearance, clearing some of the hurdles more easily for top-end microchips, and everyone knew how easily he breezed through even the hardest tests.

While no one knew quite how the chipping centers chose the order for students to go in, and there were occasional surprises based on particular pressing needs, for the most part, the highest security level chips went first. These were the lunar colony engineers, the political science specialists, military officers-to-be, and high-end programmers. Everyone figured Scott's aptitudes were likely to put him in with the first or last of those, and Mina and Miko preferred the last.

"But even if you don't expect to be with us when this is done, take down the assignment anyway, and I'll be optimistic about my chances of receiving it," Mr. Phelps continued. "In the vein we've been working on, this week's assignment is a six-page paper on how history continues to affect our lives. Since our seniors all have their chipping dates in mind, let's be a little more specific. There's bound to be some surprises, of course, but a lot of you, by now, probably have some idea what you're going to end up doing for the rest of your lives."

It was a reasonable statement. By senior year, almost everyone had been through all of the possible aptitude tests, with any talents or affinities that might help contribute to their future jobs already decided or found out. The last year was mostly for general subjects that the national education and chipping boards determined were essential for everyone, like history and the various social interaction courses at their most advanced levels. It was also a time for precise specification of assignment and for double-checking, now at the age where any hidden physical talents able to emerge would have. The latter had been Mina's primary hope for some time. A few latent genes might kick in from the other side of the family. Even just an inch or two, and she thought she might be able to make up for the rest with effort and top marks in all of her physical education classes.

"With that in mind," he went on. "The Decimation event, just a little over a century ago—how did it impact your career? And no cheating— your career specifically, not just 'It rocketed skill-chips from experiments to a basis of society,' people. Someone tries that every year; it will get an 'F'."

Half the class groaned. Miko, on the other hand, was already intently typing away. Mina stared at her screen a few moments, then became one of the people raising their hands. Mr. Phelps took a moment to draw up her student file in his chipped knowledge base, then pointed her way. "Miss Cortez?"

"What if... it doesn't? If you can't really see any impact?" she asked hopefully.

With a couple more seconds to find the right information in her file, the teacher smiled. "Your parents own Emerald City Flowers and Design, don't they? Carried on from your maternal grandfather... and your great-grandparents, right? Don't they consult on the park restoration projects? Plus, some of the flowers you still use were probably strains and hybrids designed to survive the environmental changes with less sunlight and fresh water available, right? You could do something with any of that."

Mina sunk down in her chair. It wasn't that she hadn't thought of any of that. It just wasn't the career she had been referring to. But when even her history teacher knew she was all set to become a lifelong florist, she had to admit it.

She was doomed.

Chapter Two

After school, Mina and Miko got to dance class on time. "You rush more now than for school. Trying to avoid a repeat of the Great Mrs. Bateman Scolding of 2151?"

"Plus I didn't beg and borrow every shred of time my parents would give me for dance and workouts just to miss something." Mina did what she could to support the family shop, but she was trying to remain optimistic to the last possible minute that she might still have some chance at hitting the aptitudes necessary to be accepted to a ballet academy and get chipped appropriately. Still, only Miko seemed to really keep up hope. No one, including Mrs. Bateman, who was one of the best teachers in the area, questioned Mina's work ethic or fitness. The problem had always been, simply, that in addition to physical fitness, reflexes, and precision, dancers tended towards a certain body type, and Mina's short, stocky build wasn't it.

Miko was always there for moral support. To do so, she'd managed to wedge yet another extracurricular between her piano lessons, violin lessons, history lessons, martial arts lessons, language lessons, automotive restoration research, and school. After the loss of his wife, Dr. Kimura had replaced the various family projects he had shared with his daughter with simply more classes. Still, she made time for dance to make time for Mina.

A familiar shampoo with heavy citrus notes hit Mina just as she took her place at the barre. Mrs. Bateman approached and called her aside, instructing the understudy to take Mina's place in the recital practice. At first, Mina was somewhat confused. She'd been working hard on this presentation, even with chipping coming up. After all, either of her careers—the likely, or the one she had been hoping for most of her life—were not exactly considered high priority, so she didn't expect to be anywhere in the early chipping dates. If this was to be her last presentation, she wanted to put everything she could into it, and prove that Mrs. Bateman had been right to promote her to the head of the class last year.

"Miss Cortez..." the teacher began quietly, "I'm so sorry to hear we're losing you. I only wish it were to one of the dance academies."

Mina deflated almost instantly. She had no longer been expecting to be accepted, of course, but to actually hear it took the wind out of her sails. "Can I at least work through to the production?" she asked hopefully. If nothing else, it would mean she could keep putting off full-time after-school work at Emerald City Flowers and Design. She could pretend a little longer that someone had made a mistake. Plus, of course, she'd put in a lot of work towards this presentation already.

"Well you can stay as long as you can to help your understudy, but with your chipping date before the recital—wait, you did know about your early chip date, didn't you?" Mrs. Bateman asked.

Mina looked a little startled at the news, shaking her head. "There has to be some mistake, it's just a..."

Mrs. Bateman smiled, if a bit ruefully. "They were quite specific. It may just be a review or something. If that's the case, feel free to get a pass sent to the school from the center and we'll be happy to let you back into your spot. In the meanwhile, I have to go on the information that I've been provided."

Mina sighed. "Yes, Mrs. Bateman. Thank you for trying." She meant it.

Getting through the rest of the practice wasn't as hard as she'd first imagined it to be. As long as she had something to keep her mind occupied, she was fine. It was later, after she was able to retreat away from most of the class in the locker room, that the tears hit her. Miko found her a matter of seconds later and just hugged her. She wasn't sure how long they stood like that, but she finally pulled herself together enough to finish getting dressed and head back out to the studio.

"Hey, you all right?" came Scott's voice. He wasn't any kind of dancer—or even coordinated—but he ran the dance class's computerized sound and light systems, because Mouseketeers had to stick together. While he usually got dropped off for school in the mornings with his parents going past, getting rides home from Miko got him home in time to watch his little sister almost as well as the bus did, which was all his parents tended to care about as far as priorities.

"Not exactly, but I'll tell you about it on the way to the shop..." A pause, checking her chronometer. "And I'm going to be in so much trouble," she added. Dance was provisional as it was, dependent upon her getting to work on time. While Jim and Carmen Cortez knew their daughter's ambitions, of course, they tended to be more focused on the needs of the shop ever since business had taken off. She could only guess that as soon as they found out that the class had no more practical application, she'd have to fight over being able to stay on until her chipping date to help out Miko and her understudy.

She could really only think of one thing as they worked to load Scott's tech stuff into the back of Vlad and then, worse, fold Scott himself into the car, before they took off, with Miko doing her best to bend the laws of time to get Mina to work five minutes ago.

Yeah, she was doomed.

* * * *

While not quite a success on Miko's part, with some judicious use of back roads and careful breaking of the speed laws most cars were programmed to stick to, she managed to get dropped off only a few minutes behind schedule. "Sorry I'm late," she said as she rushed into the shop.

"Mail is in—something for you," Carmen Cortez called, without looking up from her lily arrangement as Mina raced in the door. "Chipping center, I think, but no time for that. Get your shirt and jacket on, there's four deliveries lined up. They're all in the fridge unit. When you get back, you can help with inventory. Late night again. We'll have dinner ordered for you when you get back."

"With four deliveries, can I use the van?" Mina asked hopefully.

"Your dad has the van. He's working on a project with the Unitarian church. Get going," came the answer, still without looking up.

"Yes, Mother," she replied, disappointed but unsurprised. By now, it was almost routine. She looked a little despairingly at the central computer unit, but obeyed her mother, forgoing satisfying her curiosity about why the chipping center would want her in sooner rather than later. Heading into the back, she quickly changed her shirt and pulled the company jacket on, before racing to the fridge unit, drawing out the wrapped arrangements for delivery, two in cold boxes and two bouquets. She wrangled everything into a large wire basket and fit it onto the front of her bike, before heading out for the deliveries, having to race to make a couple of them on time. She was already late in the door. It would be worse if any of the deliveries were actually off schedule.

When she finally returned, sweaty from the quick exertion of deliveries right after dance class, she was hit with the scent of fresh-cut greenery as her father met her at the shop door. "You have mail!"

She was a little startled, but headed for the computer system.

"This is a big deal," Jim Cortez continued. "This will all be yours someday. Best to find out when you'll get the management programs and all so you can start learning the individual systems."

Mina shot her father a look. While they had, of course, assumed she'd be taking up the family business ever since she was born—and all the more after early aptitude tests gave her extreme marks for color spectrum recognition and her oversensitive sense of smell—they weren't supposed to refer to it. At least until it was certain.

Like now, she reminded herself. Still, she had to at least bring up her usual objections. "The presentation is in a month and a half. I was hoping to stay on with dance until then."

"Mina, we've discussed this, honey. We really need you here. We have the pre-Spring inventory coming up, and then there's all of the park work I'm going to be doing. I know that this is important to you, but if we're getting the notice already, it means you at least have a career review coming up," he replied.

"It's just until the—"

"You have an understudy. We just got a lot of new orders in. The park projects got some new donors, so we're going to have our work cut out for us. So much they may have just moved you up in priority. So take a look: is it a review, or what?"

Mina sat down heavily, pulling up the mail with a lot less anticipation one way or another than she'd had. With no real chance of anything but assignment to the flower shop, it hardly mattered much when her date was.

"Week and a half," she finally said. "And it's just a review, but they may shift my chipping date based on it," she explained, reading off the mail.

Her parents exchanged pleased glances, before her mother chimed in. "Oh, honey, the Szachs invited us to a celebration dinner this weekend. Scott will be going in first thing next week. I know that's important to you, so we arranged to shut down the shop for a couple hours... that is, provided we're all caught up on deliveries and inventory is done. You'll have to work late next two nights if we're going to get caught up."

Mina was almost expecting it at this point. "All right, I'll let Mrs. Bateman know that I won't be able to be there. Wouldn't want to miss the party." That much, at least, was true. The families hadn't gotten together outside of business for some time, and she'd want to wish Scott well. Maybe she could find out sooner if he was going to be staying local.

Trading her delivery jacket for an emerald-colored apron, Mina went into the back to start helping with shop inventory and orders.

* * * *

Dropping out of dance classes officially had been hard, and the load to catch up with work had been brutal. Despite everything, when the party approached, Mina was in decent spirits. She could be genuinely happy for Scott without any trouble.

The party was a huge affair. The Szachs were rich and had connections all over the city. Mina knew it was at the cost of never being home, between 60-hour work weeks, meetings of the various boards they sat on, and political events, but major Szach family events always filled a restaurant. In this case, it was Scott's favorite pizza place, because his preferred sandwich shop didn't have anything like the room needed. As it was, Mina couldn't help but be amused at some of the city's rich and powerful packed into a pizza parlor that usually marketed to the teen and twenty-something crowd. She was sure Benjamin and Stacy Szach would have chosen somewhere higher profile, but Scott got to pick. He'd gone for something his friends' families could easily afford, and that didn't have a dress code.

The Cortezes talked with Dr. Kimura about the newest proposals for the park project. Mina and Miko eventually went off to have dinner and conversation that didn't involve flowers and landscaping. Scott joined them as soon as he was able to get away from well-wishers, leaving his parents to handle collecting official congratulations.

As soon as he sat down, Miko pounced on the opportunity. "So?" she asked.

"You know chipping assignments are classified until all is said and done. And then, of course, even if I'd gotten something with security clearance issues, I couldn't talk about it," Scott answered.

Miko responded with a raised eyebrow, adding, "Whatever you say, Mr. Bond." Mina just grinned.

Scott glanced around, as if worried someone might be eavesdropping. Assured they had what little space could be gotten in the packed establishment, he continued. "But, you know, clearance or not, and this is strictly off the record, I could never keep a secret from you guys. I think I got it."

Chapter Three

"Officially, I'm going to be one of the lead programmers of the University's systems, working on site there. There's something more to it all, though. They're just waiting til the process is underway—and I've officially signed all their agreements, and everything is verified—to tell me all the details. Of course, if any of this comes back to me, I'd just say you guys were overexcited about a rumor, and I have no idea what anyone is talking about."

"The University?" Mina asked. "Why would you be working there? All of the chips are made out in Redmond, I thought?"

"Manufactured, sure," Scott agreed. "And I thought that too. I'm guessing with all the compatibility testing, aptitude profiling, and checking student profiles, it helps to have biology labs and student records right there. Besides, so much goes in and out of the University, what with all the computers and systems, who'd notice? I'll probably have to go out to Redmond now and then, but apparently, I'll mostly be working in some sub-sub-basement somewhere most of the time."

Miko joined Mina in grinning. "So now you get to be a professional basement troll instead of just an amateur. Excellent. They going to let you bring your video games down there? You'll never have to leave."

"Nuh-uh. And don't think I didn't ask. No outside connections. Everything, and everyone, is kept offline and totally secure."

"Okay, that is seriously impressive," Miko said, then nudged Scott with an elbow. "So, how quickly are you going to be able to hack the records and sneak Mina the ballet company assignment she got, before some clerical error mixed it up?"

14

"Miko!" Mina's grin faded, head snapping over to look Miko's way.

"Kidding, scout's honor," Miko said, holding up that three fingered sign she did every time she referenced the scouts, whoever they had been. "Mostly," she added, keeping a totally straight face.

Scott rolled his eyes. "Pretty sure everything for this cycle is done anyway. I might have to slip something extra into Miko's chip though," he assured Mina. "A love of skirts and floppy sun hats, maybe."

"Don't you dare." Miko was smirking, but one hand nevertheless clutched the brim of her fedora protectively.

"I'm sorry to interrupt," came a woman's voice from behind Mina, before a hand came to rest on her shoulder. Mina quickly processed hints of lavender shampoo and rose-scented hand soap, taking that in before she'd even turned.

The woman behind her was about average height, making her a couple inches taller than Mina, with a slightly olive complexion and gray-streaked chestnut hair that could have spoken to dozens of mixed heritages. Even with the lack of a dress code here, she wore a severe charcoal suit jacket and business skirt.

"Oh, sorry, Ma'am," Mina quickly said as she stepped aside so the woman could talk to Scott. He was the guest of honor here, after all, and doubtless would have plenty of conversations with important people in suits soon.

"Thank you, Miss Cortez, but actually I was hoping to speak with you, if you have a few moments? I'm sure your friends will understand," the woman responded, giving the other two a flash of a smile with what appeared to Mina like the well-practiced version of sincerity. "I'll be speaking more with Mr. Szach soon, but not just now."

"Mina, this is Deborah Lasko, the Deputy Mayor," Scott added in quickly. "My parents have worked with Miss Lasko on a few city projects."

Mina glanced at Scott, then back to the Deputy Mayor, confused. "To me?"

"Yes, Miss Cortez. This will only take a few moments."

"Um, sure," Mina agreed, standing from the table to follow the woman to a quieter spot near one corner of the room.

"I understand that you've got a chipping date coming up, Miss

Cortez."

"Mina is fine, Ma'am, and ... it's just a consultation. I don't think they'll be doing shops or delivery work or anything for weeks yet."

"Mina, then," the Deputy Mayor continued. "Well, you could certainly be right. Of course, it's not too late for the Bolshoi Ballet, either. If you do end up staying here, though, I know the shop has gotten a lot busier. I've just recently added the Parks and Recreation projects to my portfolio of work for the city, so I've been getting familiar with the work done by Emerald City Flowers."

"And Design," Mina added automatically. She chastised herself internally; this was awkward enough.

"Pardon me?"

"It's Emerald City Flowers and Design. Dad's side of things. The landscaping and all. Just mentioning—it really doesn't matter."

The Deputy Mayor blinked. "Oh. Right. It was just Emerald City Flowers when ... when I was much younger. At any rate, your parents have done a great job. Very impressive. I'm sure I'll be working with them—and maybe you, though I wish you luck—very closely in the near future. So I thought I'd come introduce myself."

Mina was about to respond, when she caught wind of another couple of scents. The first was expensive cologne—not out of place here at all—but against it. She thought she caught hints of metal oil and some kind of anti-corrosive. There weren't a lot of things that smell could be. Her nose twitched, and while sparing a moment to itch at it, she glanced about. She couldn't help but catch sight of a bald giant of a man, at least a couple of inches taller than the awkwardly tall Scott, but built like a brick wall to Scott's scarecrow physique. He'd edged out of the main crowd and was watching the pair of them right up until he caught Mina's glance and looked quickly away. When Mina looked back, the Deputy Mayor was frowning, though it quickly faded back to what seemed her more typical carefully neutral expression. Regardless, she said nothing about the man, and Mina decided to let that rest, though she had to wonder what else was part of the woman's civil service portfolio if she needed a bodyguard.

Mina scrambled to pick the conversation back up. "Thank you, Ma'am, I'm glad you did. We're always happy to work with the city on their projects, of course." A thought occurred, and Mina suddenly added,

"So if you've just been added on, what part interests you more, the restoration of venues to pre-Decimation looks, or the new beautification initiatives?"

This quite obviously caught the woman off-guard, and Mina had to wonder just how much work the woman had done with her parents, or how much time she'd put in studying this new area of her portfolio. She wasn't even sure why she'd asked the question, aside from just feeling that something was off, while unable to put her finger on what.

Regardless, the hint of confusion didn't last long. "Your parents' restoration work is impressive. I understand that the work done, so far, is only the beginning, though?"

"That's right, the work with the city is budgeted for at least the next five years. Dad is working with Dr. Kimura a lot on sketching out the next steps, while my mom keeps the rest of the shop business running."

"The city certainly appreciates having such a prominent archaeologist on the job. And what part of the business are you expecting to keep you busier if you work there?" the Deputy Mayor asked, shifting focus back to Mina.

"Deliveries, orders, and inventory, mostly," Mina said with a shrug, trying to keep her face and body language neutral. She appreciated the courtesy of the 'if,' at least. Unlike her father, somebody remembered not to assume.

"Ahhh, yes. I suppose those would need to be handled to keep the shop running. Good experience early on."

"Yes, ma'am. Got to get to know all parts of the business, and hopefully we'll still be working with the city when that time comes," she responded without any real enthusiasm.

"We can hope so. It's been a pleasure talking to you, Mina, but I should let you get back to your friends. This is a party, after all," the woman said, sounding genuine. Mina was left as confused as when the conversation started as to why the Deputy Mayor had wanted to talk to her in the first place.

After shaking hands with the Deputy Mayor, Mina went back to Scott and Miko, who were discussing video games as she sat back down. The conversation quickly shifted. "So what was that all about?" Miko asked.

"No clue," Mina answered, reaching for more pizza. "She asked me about the shop and my chipping date. She didn't seem to know much about any of the stuff we're doing."

"Yeah, Mom and Dad were saying it was odd," Scott said. "She suddenly added the Parks and Rec stuff to her workload, but just has some secretary attend the meetings for her and take notes."

"So, just something that got assigned to her, maybe?" Mina asked. "She certainly knew about me. She knew I was going in for a chipping consultation next week. She knew about the Bolshoi. Just felt a little weird."

"Could have been," Scott agreed. "That is kind of weird."

"So who was the huge guy staring at you two?" Miko asked.

"That's her bodyguard," Scott contributed. "Thanks to Miss Lasko's real passion. You know all those 'tough on crime' initiatives, and the big push on organized crime and getting rid of the smuggling and black-market chips into the city? Those are her babies. Those meetings she's never missed. The policeman's ball, either." Catching the glances from the others, he shrugged. "That's where I first met her, back when Mom was still on a couple of those fundraising committees and doing that neighborhood watch thing," he said between mouthfuls. "Everyone involved in city politics knows her. She's been at the job forever."

"Which is why she needs the hardcore bodyguard. Those politicians are vicious," Miko added with a grin, glancing out into the crowd again. "Bet the guy was packing heat. He had krav maga and tae kwon do, at least, chipped in."

"He was," Mina assured on the first, then raised a brow. "And just how would you know that?"

Miko grinned, dropping her voice as low as she could, managing to add a bit of gravel to it in an attempt at an impression. "It's a very distinctive stance."

Scott and Mina glanced at each other for hints of recognition, then just shook their heads.

"You guys are hopeless," Miko teased, before digging back into her pizza.

* * * *

The next few days were a blur of activity. Between some combination of whatever things he needed to sign, the chipping surgery itself, recovery time, and training, Mina didn't hear from Scott again after the party. She saw Miko at school, but otherwise most of her time was divided between work, sleep, and more work.

Mina's parents were clearly trying to make her feel more included and familiar with the business. Her father showed her layouts for park landscaping; her mother explained relations with the farms and gardens that provided supplies and inventory. Even still unchipped, Mina was handed more responsibility to arrange small orders to free up her mother to help with park work when not handling weddings, funerals, and other large-scale occasions. As expected, however, most of Mina's time was spent running deliveries. She got to use the van for bigger orders more often, but a lot of time was still spent on her bike, with three or four jobs at a time.

The end of the week neared, and her consultation loomed. She might almost have looked forward to the impending break in the routine, but the nerves just got worse. All thoughts of her chipping and the rest went out the window, however, when she returned from a delivery to find her parents waiting for her. Her mother's eyes were red from crying, while her father was in the midst of getting everything into the refrigeration unit and closing down the shop.

She had barely begun asking what happened when her mother ran up to her on Mina's way in through the door. She was pulled into a big hug. "Oh, honey ..." he mother started. "Stacy Szach just called. We're going over there now ... something's happened to Scott."

Chapter Four

The drive over to the Szachs' home was quiet.

"So what happened?" Mina asked.

"We don't know," Jim Cortez said quietly. "But Ben and Stacy are both home in the middle of the afternoon, and they need us."

Mina understood his point. The Szachs didn't come home before dusk lightly. This was serious. All sorts of scenarios ran through her head, but she forced herself to stop asking for information she knew her parents didn't have. The ride seemed to take forever, and she found herself wishing for Miko and Vlad's ability to break the posted speed limits in an emergency.

When they arrived at the Szachs' home, both of the Kimuras' cars were parked out front, along with two police cars. One officer was posted out by them, another at the door. The officer near the street talked with Mina's father a few moments, verifying who they were and that they were expected, and even scanned his wrist unit to verify his identity before letting them fully park. A few words into a subvocal mic, and the policeman at the door nodded, waving them up.

Dr. Kimura met them at the door, looking to Mina's parents and shaking his head. "No news," he started off, quietly. "Amiko is downstairs, watching Elizabeth," he told Mina.

The invitation to go join Miko with Scott's little sister was obvious, but Mina shook her head. She wanted to find out what was going on from as official a source as was available before getting Miko's understanding of the situation. She needed to have the facts to get herself grounded before Miko made it ... real. She followed along with her parents. As soon as they hit the living room, Mina's mother ran over to where Mrs. Szach was sitting on a couch, giving her a long hug before sitting down next to her. Mr. Szach was still standing when they entered, pausing from talking with two more officers as the group entered. Dr. Kimura made his way over to the standing group, followed by Mina's father. Mina settled awkwardly into one of the recliners, waiting for someone to say something.

While it was able to dispel a lot of her worst fears, the explanation raised almost as many questions. Apparently, Scott was working at the University. Officially, doing programming for the University itself, though Mina wondered. At some point, some type of kidnappers had broken into his work area. There were no official reports on what, if anything else, had been taken. The officers answered Dr. Kimura's specific questions about University security, cameras, and other measures evasively. As far as anyone could gather, the people who broke in either knew the right codes, or had managed to hack the systems, and knew where the cameras and security were stationed. Scott and most of his co-workers had disappeared from their computer lab. Beyond this, and being there to wait for an expected call from kidnappers, they didn't seem to know much—at least they wouldn't, perhaps couldn't, say much.

"Once again, Mrs. Szach, Mr. Szach, while there were signs of violence found, every indicator we have is that Scott is still alive and hopefully unhurt," an officer said. "We're keeping a security detail here, and the house phones are ready to trace any ransom calls that come in. We have people still investigating at the University." It seemed to be a refrain.

Despite her frustration with the situation and lack of answers, she couldn't help but feel for the policemen's position. Having to be the bearers of that kind of news, while not having any kind of reason or logic to offer frantic parents, or worse, having information that might help something like this make sense, but not being able to share it, even with those parents.

Mina was sitting there, simply thinking about that professional situation. She sat there while the parents talked quietly, almost like they did in the 'pre-shindigs.' Any minute now, someone would go get the veggie tray, just to test it out.

Except that didn't make any sense. Not because they were talking to police officers, but because the bringing out of the veggie tray had to be accompanied by Mrs. Kimura's playful cursing of her doctors for forbidding blue cheese dressing. The three families hadn't really had a 'pre-shindig' since Mrs. Kimura died. Just the official parties, just business. And now, just ... this. Missing the professor's wife jarred her abruptly back to what the conversation was about.

She quickly excused herself, feeling a bit dizzy and disconnected. On her way down into the cool basement, something in her brain didn't give up trying to convince her that none of this could be real. Scott would be downstairs, with his video games plugged into his eye, while Miko would be showing Beth ancient TV series or movies.

She found the pair of girls on the couch of the downstairs TV room. Scott's room door was open, but the computer was turned off, the chair unoccupied, connection wires dangling loose from the desk. Miko was, indeed, using her hand-held vid player to show some series or other, but she wasn't doing any of the voices, or adding little quips and bits of the history of the show while they watched. A little under a year ago, when she was still eight, Beth had decided she was too old for her stuffed animals and dolls and had packed most of them away. Now she was half-wrapped around the teddy bear that Miko had won her at the state fair baseball toss (and let Scott claim credit). Miko had even lent Beth her fedora, making her very red eyes all the more visible.

At the sound of Mina's entry, both girls disentangled themselves and ran to her, leaving the hand-held running in front of the bear. Miko buried her head on Mina's shoulder and wrapped her arms around her, while Beth did her best to encircle both girls' waists.

It was only then that everything came crashing down to the level of reality, and Mina started crying too.

* * * *

No news and no ransom calls came in the days following, but at least there was also no sign of bodies or anything that would signal the worst. The police were still operating under the theory of kidnapping for ransom. The Szachs had received a long line of the city's elite wishing them well and offering any help they could provide. The police were a constant presence, and Beth was given a security escort to school. The Cortezes and

Kimuras were there almost every night after work, but work had to go on. Scott was missing, and Mina was delivering flowers.

Aside from the responsibilities of work, she had this consultation or whatever it was. She'd been dreading this even before all of the chaos with Scott. Now she was just wishing it could be delayed indefinitely. Still, when the day arrived, there she was. With Miko, thank goodness.

"Are you sure you don't need me to give you a ride?" her mother had asked. "I can leave your dad alone with the shop for a while when it's your Chipping Day!" Carmen Cortez was excited.

"Thanks Mom, but it's not my Chipping Day. Just one of those special consideration meetings they mentioned in school." Implanting someone with everything they needed to know to do their assigned job perfectly had become a mostly exact science in the century-and-some it had been in use, but complications still came up. "Dr. Kimura got Miko out of school for the day. I'll be fine." Mina wouldn't have been able to bear her mother's excitement over Mina's florist chip.

The chipping center in Bellevue loomed. Mina had seen the place before, with its odd mixture of hospital and militarized zone. Heavy security patrolled the grounds, and they had to go through two different checkpoints to get in. This part of the process, at least, Mina understood perfectly. With the right chip, someone could do or learn almost anything. The black market was huge.

Miko sighed as they went through the first security line. "Gotta make sure we're not here to fry ourselves trying to become billionaire astrophysicist racecar drivers," she whispered.

Mina got the joke even if she didn't really smile properly. Just as big as the potential benefits of black-market chipping were the risks. Chips were directly tied in to a person's aptitudes. While a chip technically provided all the knowledge—and even rote muscle memory and reactions—to do a job, a person's interests and physical suitability to the tasks still played a part. And 'interests' were not always the same as 'goals.' A chip might give an ambitious buyer perfect knowledge of human anatomy and perfect reactions to deal with every mishap that might arise. If, however, the recipient didn't already have perfectly steady hands and a curiosity regarding the connections of muscles, nerves and organs, the chances of a surgeon's chip malfunctioning went up exponentially.

23

Hundreds of thousands of people had faced neurological damage or death in the evolution of the battery of physical and psychological tests, surveys, and interviews to determine that Mina was, in fact, absolutely perfect to a lifetime of working with flowers. Somehow, their sacrifices didn't inspire her to any greater enthusiasm about the prospect.

The first checkpoint let them into the overall installation. Each of the centers in the two-square-mile complex would be dealing with different aspects of the work being done. Mina was directed towards the overflow building. This is where they'd take oddities being handled outside the normal schedule, like emergency florists. The place wasn't terribly busy, but most of the parking spots were built for modern, minimalist cars, not archaic monsters like Vlad. They ended up parking amidst a few vans and work vehicles, then made the trek to the building.

"I have the day off," Miko reminded her, a hand on Mina's shoulder. "So I'll be here to take you to the shop or home or whatever you need."

Mina didn't respond at first, just looking up at the block-long, severe-looking building with its metal walls and security checkpoint at the doors. At first, the two guards stationed there were hesitant to let a non-family member through, but a short debate, a brief scan of her subdermal ID chip, and a review of Dr. Kimura's project clearance and status got her waved through after a few minutes and a supervisor's approval.

"Glad that's settled. They weren't getting rid of me so easily, and now we don't have to figure out if we could've taken them," Miko whispered cheerily.

"What do you mean, 'we'? You and your aikido-tae-kwon-do-krav-maga would be on your own." Mina tried to smile this time, but it was wry at best. She didn't know any of that stuff because she was a one-hobby girl, and didn't even have that one anymore.

Miko rolled her eyes dramatically. "Pft, My aikido-tae-kwon-do-wushu-krav-maga. You forgot one. And tai chi, but that's more a morning exercise program before piano lessons. After. I mean, after. It was before … before. Still, bet we could have taken them."

Most of the descriptions of Chipping Days Mina had been given were of parking lots full of vehicles from the nearest seven states and packed hallways that eventually let people into equally packed waiting rooms. From the traffic, she suspected several of the other buildings were dealing with that, but this building was mostly quiet. Three other families had staked out their own areas of the sterile waiting room decorated only with charts, lists, and places to tack up more charts and lists. A few nurses and orderlies moved about from place to place, but it was nothing like the chaos she'd envisioned.

Mina and Miko found two seats with a bit of distance. All the other kids had family along. A redheaded—copper-haired, really—girl sat in near silence next to her mother. The girl chewed nervously on her nails every time her mother looked back down into her magazine. Mina matched a second family to a van with Montana license plates near where they'd parked. She figured she could be wrong, but word around Seattle always had it that you could tell the country kids and people who'd had the long trips to get there. They were the ones who dressed really nicely for the day at the center. All the people from close enough to have made a few trips by the center supposedly knew to dress as comfortably as possible, because everyone was going to be there a while. The big, muscular boy and his parents were all a lot more tanned than most of the locals managed to get anyway.

The last group were providing most of the noise in the place. While the other families talked quietly, a woman in a University of Oregon sweatshirt worked hard to run herd on a small, short-haired blond boy, who wanted to explore everything. Climbing and crawling on and amidst chairs and side tables, he prompted his mother to drag him back to her immediate presence every few minutes. A girl who Mina figured was probably the boy's twin sister sat quietly, clutching a stuffed duck in Oregon's jungle green and tangerine yellow. Their older brother was immersed in a biology textbook while waiting, either just that bored, or engaged with the scholarly subject above and beyond chipped information. The family's father showed the signs of a long drive; he slid forward in his chair, cat napping while they waited for their son to be called.

Mina scanned every chart and list within reading distance, then scanned over the other people waiting, wondering why they were here. Some were harder to guess than others. She started running through a few imagined scenarios in her head, filling in details with speculation and context clues. Miko was watching and knew Mina far too well. There was a comm text. *"What's the verdict?"*

25

"Okay, the Oregon Kid, I'm almost positive," Mina sent back. *"Probably some kind of university research posting."* If there was a retirement or death within staff at a major research facility, it would make sense they'd be trying to fill it quickly.

"Big guy in his rumpled Sunday's Best?"

"Don't know about Montana Kid. Montana Dad may be a trucker. Tan darker on one elbow. Arm out of window a lot? Still doesn't mean anything. Montana Kid may be luckier than I."

Aptitudes ran in families often enough that it wasn't unusual for kids to follow similar careers, but it was hardly universal. Still, Mina could imagine reasons why more transport workers might be needed in a hurry.

"Redhead?"

"I've got nothing."

The copper-haired girl looked like an awful lot of the girls in Mina's class. T-shirt and jeans, painted nails with rough edges from the nervous habit, long hair kept in a braid—nothing that readily gave a lot away. She fidgeted in silence.

'Skick!' went the sound of another bitten nail, and the mother glanced up from her magazine sternly. The girl tried to sit on her hands in reaction. Yes, there was some tension between them. Mina found her attention drawn to the mother's nails. Brightly painted, definitely a good sign she didn't do anything that was going to scuff them up. On the other hand, the woman kept them trimmed short, perhaps for typing, or maybe playing piano or something, Mina reminded herself, with a glance aside to Miko's nails, short since those lessons started at age eight. Still, she could see the woman as a secretary—about the right amount of makeup and general sense of professional style in evidence for someone used to dealing with people, used to a steady 9-to-5 career. Mina guessed that perhaps the daughter was going into something drastically different, more socially isolated or unpredictable, and the woman didn't entirely approve. Perhaps it was even that this was a consultation, and the girl didn't even know precisely what she'd be doing yet. Good reason to be nervous there as well.

She wasn't sure how long she'd been sitting there when a small voice asked, "How long's it take to make somebody a prob'ly-lab-monkey?" The tiny blonde girl wasn't talking to Mina. With her family preoccupied, she was addressing Miko with earnest concern.

"Well," Miko replied cheerfully, "It used to take years and years." Then, soothingly, as the girl's eyes widened in distress, she added, "But that was a long time ago. If this is his day, he'll know all about labs by bedtime."

"Oh."

Mina noted the correct call just a little smugly. There were no prizes, of course; it was just a habit. And better, maybe, than turning those musings on what would happen to the girl who was wearing Danskins™, but clearly didn't have the legs to be a professional ballerina.

The probably-lab-monkey got called in first. He hadn't been gone for a minute when the family decided to collect the littler ones and go find some breakfast, or maybe it was lunch. The center felt immeasurably bigger and more empty the second they'd left.

Not long after, the nurse called, "Mina Teresa Cortez."

"Excuse me," Mina said, surprised. "Did you say Mina Teresa Cortez?" After all, she'd arrived last, so she expected to be called last. The nurse verified that it was her turn and that Miko wasn't going to be permitted back with her. The nurse and desk attendant both made a note of making sure security had Miko's name and license plate though so she could get back to the building and the waiting area at any point she wanted, if she decided to leave the chipping center.

"Thanks," said Miko as she turned on her ear buds to listen to music instead.

The nurse led Mina back through a maze of hallways. She'd always had a fair sense of direction, which helped with her deliveries, but even so, she was lost within the first two minutes. The nurse navigated the center's labyrinthine ways with practiced—and probably chipped—ease, eventually showing Mina to a sterile room, this one white, in contrast to the steel gray and various shades of beige in the rest of the center. There was a padded table, a couple of countertops, and two chairs. An open metal secure box rested on the examining table.

"Please go ahead and get changed into a robe. Your clothes can go into that safebox there. Lock it up when you're done and leave it on the countertop. You'll get everything back when we check you out. Did you have any questions?"

"Wait ... so I'm actually being chipped? I thought this was just a consultation or something."

"Oh dear," the nurse answered, checking her paperwork. "Chipping Date: Mina Teresa Cortez. I can understand being nervous, honey, but it's not that big a deal. We'll have you out and walking by tonight."

Chapter Five

"No, no ... I'm not nervous. I know all that. I just ... I'm going to be working at a flower shop. It's not like ... well, not like a Week Two thing."

The Nurse shrugged. "This is the date we were given. If you'd like us to call your family, we can do that, but you're going to be in isolation through the surgery and a few follow ups. Still, if you thought it was a consultation, they should probably know. They'll want to be here when you're done."

Mina bit back the comment that they'd probably want to know when she'd be ready to go back to work first. "Okay, yeah, give them a call. Just let them know it's no big deal for now. They don't need to be here. My friend can give me a lift back home."

"Okay, I'll let them know. You're going to want to take it really easy for a few days. The procedure is minimally invasive, but we're still attaching something to your spine. It's—"

"Thank you," Mina interrupted, with a small smile. "I'm okay, really." She was sure, despite all the classes, some kids would want reassurance up til the last minute. Now that she was here, Mina just wanted to get on to the point she wouldn't need to be here any longer.

Once the nurse left, Mina quickly changed into the too-brief hospital gown. She managed to tie it reasonably well, found a pair of linen-white slippers, then shut her clothes up in the box and went to peek out of the room. "Okay, I'm ready," she called.

The nurse returned, leading her through a few more empty, maze-like, hallways and eventually to a surgical room. She met briefly with the two doctors, then the handful of additional assistants and nurses. They went through the expected battery of explanations, whether she needed them or not.

"Some people process certain kinds of knowledge better than others. Chips don't reprogram anyone," the doctor explained.

"—they just transmit electrical impulses, which translate into a certain kind of data, or encourage a certain kind of action," Mina said. "I promise I wasn't one of the ones sleeping in class."

"And you know that there's no guarantees, but the risk of chip rejection or complications has dropped to being almost negligible."

"As long as you follow proper processes and don't try and mess with your chip or try and get anything added to it," Mina continued. "I know. Most of the horror stories are at least a couple generations old, or turned out to be Black Market chips."

Mina was given another chance to ask questions, then was helped onto the padded metal table, face down. She put her face through the small hole that would let her breathe easily while undergoing surgery. They assured her the anesthesia would help her sleep through the process and not feel a thing.

She felt the shot, then continued to hear voices for a little bit, which became increasingly distant as the medicine kicked in. Her last impressions were of marks being made on her upper back and neck with a marker while the surgical crew talked. Then, though Mina still wasn't ready to wake up a florist, everything went dark.

A taste like chewing on tinfoil and a slight burning sensation somewhere in her nasal cavity woke Mina. She registered that much, felt a rush of adrenaline, and before she picked up anything else of her surroundings, she rolled off of the table. She landed in a crouch, feeling the slight constriction of sweatpants around her legs. Before she could ponder how she'd gotten a change of clothes, or why she was behind a fixed table with drawers rather than an operating table, she heard a smack of hard plastic on the tabletop where she'd been laying a split second before.

The table wouldn't last as a hiding place for long, but she had moved across the way from her potential attacker, giving her a moment. At first, she detected chaotic movement. Something in her brain raced through assessing her situation, and she smelled three others in the room—two sets of actual movement, coming around the desk from opposite sides. At least a hint of synth-skin, so probably some cybernetics somewhere.

Two masked figures came into view, rounding each side of the desk. Despite the clear threat, though she wasn't sure why, Mina's initial adrenaline-laced panic started to fade.

She tensed, head snapping forward, watching both out of her peripheral vision. As they committed themselves to trying to corner Mina, her crouch gave her the perfect start for a spring upward, hands planting on the tabletop, turning into a smooth somersault to the other side of it and onto her feet.

That was when the surreality of being attacked got even more surreal. Not from the somersault—Mina could do a somersault. That was fine. What was surreal was the way her feet shifted into one of Miko's aikido stances. She wasn't clumsily copying what she'd seen. She was falling naturally into something she'd never actually done in her life. She felt a bit like a character in one of Scott's video games, like her motions weren't entirely under her control, but whoever had the controller was doing just fine

As one of the masked men reversed field, coming back around, she stepped into him. He brought the hard plastic baton up into an attack posture. Mina continued her momentum forward, using the heavy desk as a barrier to keep the fight one on one. She closed the distance before he could get any momentum behind the swing, one hand coming up to parry the attack at his forearm instead of risking blocking the baton with her bare arm. Her other hand lashed out with an open palm strike to his solar plexus. There was a muffled thump on impact, her brain registering some kind of light body armor under his shirt that kept the blow from knocking the wind out of him.

Already adjusting his position, he tried for a sapping blow under her chin. She ducked her head back and to the side even as she registered what he was doing, the man's hand coming up a millimeter from striking. Her dodge left her in better position to follow up than her attacker. She let her momentum carry her into a full spin, dropping into a low sweep kick. Her attacker jumped over it, but his landing gave her a split second free of his press. She pushed upward again, not even looking back, just remembering where the desk was to brace herself properly, turning her backwards leap into a roll across the desktop, coming up on her feet atop the desk.

From her position on high ground, a new flurry of motion caught her attention in time to let her snap a leg out, avoiding the attack to her shin, stepping down on the baton. Her defense was jarring enough that the attacker lost hold of the baton under Mina's foot. She hooked her toes under the baton, kicking it up into the air and catching it. Now armed, she resumed her stance, trying to assess both attackers.

As Mina was about to spring off the desk toward him, they were interrupted by a firm voice. "Enough! Her chip has obviously taken fine."

Mina was startled enough that her readiness to leap almost translated into tumbling forward face-first off the desk. Instead, she felt her arm and shoulder tucking without her bidding, turning the fall into a graceful roll and perfect dismount off the desk top. She had in her mind to hit the guy who'd been swinging at her, just in case, but the same odd new reflex she'd been feeling guiding her through the action movie moves told her there was no more threat present. She almost smacked him anyway, on principle.

That urge dissipated as she finally got a look at the third person present, and immediately recognized her. The big woman from her bicycle wipe-out, with the cyber-arm. "What ...?" she stammered, eyes locked on the figure. The woman responded by gesturing to the pair of men. The one still armed set his baton down. Both removed their masks, and turned to face the woman with the cyber-arm. "There will be more tests, but you passed the most crucial one. You've accepted your chip. Welcome to the Secret Police, Miss Cortez."

"Okay, okay ... slow down ... Secret Police ... what?" Mina started, tensing up again. "Who are you people? Why did they attack me? Why am I not in the center? Why do I know aikido? Why am I dressed?" she rapid fired, tone shifting from baffled to almost accusing as she locked eyes on the big woman.

The woman looked unstirred, just waiting for Mina to finish before saying a word. "A little respect, Miss Cortez. I know this is confusing, but not half as confusing as the bigger world you're about to enter. Let's begin with this: you are presently in no danger. This may be the last time in your new life I can say that with certainty. Secondly, I am Director Fiona Richter, henceforth, either Director, Director Richter, or Ma'am while here. Outside these walls, we do not know each other. Is that clear?"

Chapter Six

Faint hints of aluminum chewing, as one part of Mina's brain told her to salute. She ignored it and stopped the twitch of her arm before it got far into the reflex motion. She also bit back any number of sarcastic comments from another part of her brain entirely. Now that the adrenaline had died down, she was having an easier time recognizing the chipped impulses and reflexes. She still couldn't imagine why she needed those kind of reflexes, but at least she knew they were there. "All right ... I mean, yes, Director," Mina answered, quickly starting to feel like she was talking to her father.

"Very good, Miss Cortez. You have been selected to receive one of the rarest chips in the world."

Mina's brain, still firing off questions rapid fire, prompted her to interrupt the Director's all-too-slow explanation. "So, wait, I got a cop chip?"

The Director's response, maddeningly, was to slow down further, just fixing Mina with a stern gaze that chased any more urge to fire off questions to the back of her mind. Towering over her, the woman suddenly seemed like she'd grown another two feet, or Mina had shrunk. As soon as Director Richter was content that she had Mina's undivided attention, she continued in deliberate fashion.

"Police chips are admirable things. I wouldn't mind seeing more people get them, but no. You're not a policewoman, though that is one of the most common and broadly useful cover identities used in our line of work. You're now a deep-cover spy, of sorts. Inserted into the normal population with a complex chip capable of helping you with your other career. When called upon for assignment, you'll engage in espionage, high-level city security activities, counter-terrorism work, and the occasional black market investigation when it goes above the police's heads. You have a license to work within any of the nations signed on to the security agreement, as well as the necessary language skills, but will primarily be quartered here in Seattle."

Mina blinked. There was a pause, then it grew longer while Mina absorbed some of what she was being told. She realized that the Director was awaiting some acknowledgment she understood, and the next question, along with a gaze that said that the next question had better be a very good one. "So ..." she started, "I'm not going to be running the flower shop? All my aptitude tests said I'd be perfect for, you know, selling flowers ... "She immediately felt like an idiot as the words left her mouth.

The Director's tone stayed even. "Well, yes, your file suggested you would be an excellent florist ... except the part in your psych profile that indicated that you'd snap within 5 years. Same reason we end up having to be so careful with postal worker and air traffic controller chips." If that was a joke, the woman wasn't laughing.

After a brief pause, she continued. "However, you will still be selling and delivering flowers. As far as your parents or most of the city are concerned, you are a delivery girl, chipped to eventually take over your parents' business. We could think of no better cover than someone who has an excuse to be absolutely anywhere at almost any time. We just have to call and place an order, and you have an excuse to be away for variable amounts of time. Many of the chip routines are also similar: perfect city maps, multiple programmed languages, and so on."

Mina just nodded along, before the words actually registered fully. "So ... wait ... I'm a spy ... and a secret cop ... and whatever else ... and my parents still get to make me do inventory?"

The Director raised a brow. "Something like that. Though you have a significant expense account, suitable to your pay grade, you will be expected to live within your cover identity's means. No fancy car, no buying a house tomorrow, and due to risks of spies being compromised, very limited vacations. However, be assured, you'll someday be able to retire very comfortably. You will be expected to live up to the expectations of your cover: inventory, deliveries, sales ... everything you'd do otherwise. 80 to 90 percent of the time, that will be the extent of your work, in ideal circumstances. It needs to be believable over a wide span of years. Be assured, however, that does not make what you're actually doing any less important. During the remaining ten to twenty percent of your time, you will be helping to save the world as we know it—no exaggeration."

Mina thought about it a few moments. Aside from the flower delivery part, it sounded kind of exciting. Besides, she supposed she'd have plenty of things to think on while running inventory or checking receipts. In any case, this didn't sound like the sort of job you turned down." So ... who can I tell about all of this, exactly?"

"The people in this room, the Deputy Mayor and her entourage, and other individuals we specify. Your chip has clearance levels programmed in. You'll be able to recognize the handful of authorized people, and it will give you a warning if you're about to say something you shouldn't to anyone else."

"So, my parents—"

"Are not to know anything. Your maternal grandfather didn't tell his daughter, and neither of their psych profiles suggest they would take it very well.

"A—" Mina attempted to interrupt, but the woman spoke right on through.

"When we need you, we'll arrange reasons for you to be out of the shop for as much time as needed. Right now, for example, there's a complication with your chipping, and you're under observation. That will go on through your meeting with the Deputy Mayor.

"But A—" Mina tried again. The Director was having none of it.

"You will have regular deliveries to make in the mornings for some time. Primarily, this will give us time to introduce you to your first assignment. It will also let us work on your physical training." Finally, when Mina was giving up on getting the question in, Director Richter affirmed, "Yes, your maternal grandfather was one of our agents. The shop still has a couple of hidden areas. It had the advantage of being one of those rare places anyone could reasonably walk into without drawing attention, and few people tend to associate flower shops with spycraft."

Mina blinked several times. A bit of additional motion to one side drew her attention, snapping her back to the realization the other people, still all in black, but no longer masked, were still flanking her. To her left was a tall, thin man, now revealed to be perhaps a few years older than her parents, with hints of mixed Asian ancestry of some sort.

"Your grandfather taught me everything I know about the job. He was a good man," he said, with an easy smile. "Now I get to return the favor. You'll be reporting in to me tomorrow, and I'll get you all caught up and start your training."

"What kind of training, exactly?" Mina asked, directing it vaguely between the older man and the Director, for whoever cared to answer, finding herself hoping her new trainer would be the one to field it.

No such luck, the Director took the initiative again. "Part of the selection process for agents is physical ability. Every agent tests in the top percentiles in numerous areas. Endurance, fitness, ability to push themselves—trying to get into a top ballet academy has served you well. You pushed yourself to the top of the toughest dance program in your price range. You then biked a dozen miles at a time through the hills on deliveries. It was enough to get you in the door. Now we're going to take that potential and push it to its limits. You'll be trained to ambidexterity. Get as comfortable with backwards or lateral movement either direction as normal walking. There will be overspeed training. Most importantly, we'll be coaching up your fast-twitch muscles. The chip in your spine lets you react as close to the speed of thought as your body is physically capable. Your reaction to Agents Park and Hall showed that to be reasonably capable, but your muscles are still unused to this kind of action. We need to improve on that speed, and we will."

Agent Park, she guessed, was nodding to one side. Mina wasn't entirely sure she liked the look of his expression, and could already start to feel the burn in her muscles. She was positive she didn't like the look on the Director's face though, so she still thought it preferable.

A glance, at last, in her other direction, and Mina's heart skipped a beat. She hadn't dated much in school. That would have taken time from work—not an option—or dance class, equally non-negotiable as far as Mina herself was concerned. She did know the boys she had seen here and there for school functions weren't really her type, and she'd tried to just not worry too much about it. (It had helped that, even at the worst of the boy-crazy phases of most of her friends and classmates, Miko had continued to profess that the only guy she had the vaguest hint of a crush on was John Belushi, whoever that was.) Whatever defined her type, though, she was pretty sure Agent Hall was it. Tall, dark, just a little rugged. Maybe four or five years older than she was. Mina felt a slight heat, her cheeks coloring, and tried to bring herself back to the seriousness of the situation. Thankfully, or unfortunately, the Director's stern gaze did wonders for dragging her back to the moment.

"Now, the initial test is done, and my comm just told me the Deputy Mayor has arrived to meet our newest agent. I'm sure she'll be happy to take the rest of your questions," she told Mina. Left unsaid, but clear, nonetheless, was anything about exactly how unhappy the Director was to be being pulled away from her workload to answer rookie questions at all. "Agent Park, can you show Agent Cortez to the meeting room and help her get acclimated?"

Agent Park—the older man, as she'd guessed—quickly agreed, much as Mina found herself wishing it was Agent Hall helping her get acclimated. Even so, she was hating this less and less by the moment.

Chapter Seven

"So these are the Seattle FBI offices? Quite a drive from the Bellevue chipping center," Mina remarked during the short tour of the building she'd awoken in. It was going much better than the previous conversation.

Agent Park nodded. "Your doctors and nurses were cleared to handle the sensitive information chips. Once you were safe to move, the nurses got you dressed and loaded into a refitted police transport truck, sort of half-ambulance."

It was nice to get reasonably sensible answers to her initial questions. "And it's okay to just go anywhere in this place?"

"Technically, yes. Don't let any of the FBI staff get too used to you, though. Agents, civilians, anybody. Except, obviously, Director Richter. Her day job is here."

"That's probably convenient for her, right?"

"Yes. It lets her monitor federal investigations, stuff that connects to the bigger job."

"And you? And, um, Agent Hall?" She told herself not to blush.

"Police detectives," he said, not letting on if he noticed the blushing or not as they walked to a particularly quiet part of the building. "This bit here is our corner, for when we all actually do have to meet in person. Director Richter's office, a couple of typically empty meeting rooms, and a temp office for the Deputy Mayor, 'just to coordinate with various authorities for the city's Security Commission,' you know." The older man's tone grew lighter and drier as he pointed out the appropriate doors.

Mina recognized the tone as referencing an apparent cover story. She was clearly going to have to get used to a lot of those. "So what about the part of that I don't know?" Mina asked.

"More of a question for Miss Lasko herself," Agent Park said, smiling. "Now, the next part of the rundown. I want you to think of St. Joshua's medical clinic."

At the request, Mina picked up on that hint of aluminum that she was beginning to associate with her chip kicking in. The name of the clinic triggered five different routes to get there, along with the uses of each route. One was fastest. Another let her avoid cameras. One was only accessible by foot or bicycle at several points. Eventually, it settled on a combination of the address, and knowledge of precisely whom to talk to and what to say to be allowed into the elevator to the basement.

"Training facilities for tomorrow are in the clinic basement. It's one of several safehouses we've got available to us in the city." Park continued outlining the usual plan for getting her to such places. She'd get a call for delivery to any of a number of locations at the far end of the usual 'biking range,' or a series of closer deliveries. Either way would justify a couple of hours. Her tracking comm implant had already been rigged so that she could appear to be anywhere she wanted within the region, should her parents check up on her progress, or if Miko were looking for her.

"Fortunately, the whole 'medical complications' excuse that's covering for you here now should prevent your parents being too surprised, these next couple days, if you come back more out of breath, or don't quite hide the stiffness properly when you walk."

"Oh, that doesn't sound ominous," Mina remarked ironically at the implication for her initial physical training.

"It didn't? I must not have said it right," he said with just a hint of a smile. "We're going to be thorough, Cortez. From the sound of things, you're enough like your grandfather that you wouldn't settle for less even if we would." More of a smile. "Which we won't."

"So his car accident—"

Agent Park sighed slightly. "I think you can guess what kind of 'car accident' it was, but that's also more of a question for the Deputy Mayor. Today or a day like it, obviously, not during everyday life."

"This stuff and everyday life ... it's a little bit of cognitive dissonance."

"Yeah. The Inquisitor angle—" At Mina's sudden eyebrows, Agent Park clarified with a sheepish gesture. "The organization, 'this stuff'—it will bring some big cases. Sometimes very big: international crime syndicates, black marketeers, and human trafficking. Most of the time, though, I'm a cop. You're a florist."

Mina nodded. But the big stuff colored everything else, really. Even deliveries would be part of her chance to do something important. Which reminded her. "The Director mentioned a first case. What is it?"

Agent Park sighed. "That's not really a question for me either," he answered, before urging her towards her next meeting before she inquired further.

There was a lot she was still confused about, but she was feeling better about the situation in general. Suspicions about the veracity of any of this cropped up now and then, but her earlier encounter with the Director amidst a police investigation helped. She was able to confirm pretty easily that they were at the FBI building. Likewise, while still uneasy with being kidnapped at all, she was positive that anyone able to kidnap someone from the chipping center had to have some pretty high level clearance.

Now, they were willingly dragging her before one of the city's longest-serving officials. While it was further evidence the 'secret police' were legitimate, that meeting still made her nervous. She was pretty sure she wasn't on the Deputy Mayor's list of favorites after their meeting at Scott's party. Just standing in front of the door, that growing comfort from Agent Park's easygoing frankness suddenly dissipated.

* * * *

Whatever she was expecting, it wasn't the friendly greeting she received. The Deputy Mayor met her at the door. The big man Mina had seen at the party was settled onto a couch to one side of the office, along with a much smaller Japanese man in a similar suit. Where before, she had had to wait for the hint of gun oil to guess at the man's being armed, now tiny telltale signs raced through her brain, sizing both men up for armament, combat readiness and state of alertness, and that was with little beyond a cursory glance.

That glance was all she got before the Deputy Mayor all but hugged her. "Mina! It's wonderful to see you again. I'm so sorry for the awkwardness at the party. Despite all of your marks, no one was quite certain about you as an agent. It's a lot of tough criteria, and not very many people are suited for it."

"So, are you one of the Secret Police?" Mina asked. Her chip gave her the all clear on talking to the woman, at least.

"Oh, no. At least not as an agent. I'm a political liaison. While I have a lot of responsibilities, one of the big ones, at least as concerns your organization, is to make sure that the city, state, and federal authorities aren't in your way, and coordinate with you when necessary."

Mina blinked a couple times. "Federal? So ... where, exactly, do we rank compared to the FBI? The Director mentioned multinational work."

The Deputy Mayor nodded. "You'll work with select agents sometimes, if they get sufficient clearance to know that some of you are undercover, though they never know precisely who you're undercover with." Mina could sympathize. Miss Lasko continued. "Please come and have a seat, and I'll give you the standard history lesson."

Mina started towards the desk. "You do this a lot, um, Ma'am?"

"Please, Mina, call me Deborah," she said, then shook her head. "Not as much as I used to. Certainly not as much as my predecessor. The role of your organization has been steadily decreasing with each generation." she explained, as she moved to the other side of the desk.

"So there used to be more than ... what, four of us in the city?" Mina checked, trying to get a sense of what size organization she was a part of.

She nodded. "In your grandfather's day, there were quite a few just in Seattle. Now, there are, yes, less than half a dozen normal agents, a few contacts who know part of the story, and a few emergency contacts.

The allied governments are paying a lot of money for each fully chipped agent to be doing another job. In some cases, where they're still doing police or security work, the politicians who know what's going on are more easily convinced that it's still a worthwhile investment.

Police have strict limitations that private investigators don't, though, and then there's all the delivery people, people who run import/export companies, translators, private chefs, wine tasters, and others whose jobs give them excuses to end up in sensitive places or getting close to just the right people. Instead of grasping that, the paper-pushers just see expensive chips and salaries for everyday jobs and don't want any more."

Mina settled in, considering the Deputy Mayor. "So ... my organization, the secret police, the ....Inquisition? We work with the FBI, but we're not part of them. It's been around since my grandfather, but ... I'm still missing a lot of details here. What organization am I working for, exactly?"

The Deputy Mayor nodded. "Ultimately, you're the Allied Investigative Agency, or AIA. A multinational organization with broad investigative powers.

"I'm not an expert on that sort of thing," Mina said carefully, "But aren't limits actually a good thing for ... secret police?"

"I know the term often makes for images of brute squads, people disappearing in the middle of the night and Big Brother listening in on every word... " Deborah Lasko smiled, her hands in a 'but wait' style of gesture. "This organization is tied to no one country or regime, does not support or oppose any political party, and only gets involved with high profile organized crime and similar concerns. The program only selects agents with psych profiles with the highest scores as far as personal integrity and responsibility."

Mina managed a sheepish smile. It was a little flattering, certainly. Some of the commentary still made her uneasy, but she was glad to hear that there was at least some kind of checks in place.

"Historically, the AIA have always tried to intrude on the day-to-day lives of most people as little as possible, aside from keeping them safer from multinational cartels and threats on a similar scale."

"Historically?" Mina was glad for the opening.

Miss Lasko settled back in her chair a bit, Mina taking her easy smile as approval of the general line of thought. "It started after the Decimation Event. After the supervolcano in the American Midwest, there was almost no sunlight for a year and a half. Earthquakes, floods, armies of refugees. No one was prepared for a disaster on that scale. Uncontaminated drinking water was going for fine wine prices in some regions. Survival necessitated international cooperation on a massive scale. Problem was, it took a lot of people a long time to realize it. Wars broke out—everyone wanted organization to be on their terms. Eventually, though, there were enough food riots, coups, and real threats that the bullying and flag-waving stopped and negotiation started."

Mina listened and nodded. "But those were trade and aid agreements, to get food and whatever from wherever anyone found sunlight or new farming stuff. How did ...?"

"The problem afterwards was simply that no one trusted each other. The United States and China, in particular, had a great deal of trouble dealing with each other on a diplomatic basis. Combined with rampant organized crime and the black market having boomed, and the whole process threatened to fall apart."

Mina reflected that Miko would probably have some interesting commentary on all this. She decided it was best not to ponder any of this coming up to Miko, and continued listening.

"England managed to bring together a number of nations with reasonably good diplomatic relations. The purpose of the AIA was to monitor some of the heavy international travel and trade for signs of black marketeers, enemy spies, and signs that other nations weren't holding up their end of the deal. Unlike most of the security agencies who worked within only one nation, the agents were given broad rights across the alliance. There were no central offices, no acknowledgment that the organization existed, or anything for the political machine to latch onto and start legislating. There were abuses of power. The AIA's early history was occasionally ugly, and not that dissimilar to that of most top-secret programs with little limitation on their power."

Mina was a little shocked that the woman so readily admitted the abuses. She wasn't whitewashing the AIA's history, and she definitely didn't seem to be glorifying the United States' role in things. Miss Lasko continued to surprise her. She nodded her understanding, gesturing for the Deputy Mayor ... Deborah ... to continue.

"But the AIA eventually instituted strict rules for the recruitment of agents based upon psychological profiles. Worked right alongside the evolution of chipping, really. The world was in desperate need of more doctors and farmers, fast. Various agencies, meanwhile, needed loyal agents who were up to their high standards. At that point, the AIA had people everywhere, particularly among the crowds of refugees, merchants, and aid workers. With a more responsible AIA hiring policy, the abuses of power dropped drastically. The less people had to worry about the secret police, the less anyone wanted to believe in such an unpleasant-sounding thing."

"So they ... disappeared into skepticism?"

"Pretty much. They adopted a strict policy of not interfering in anything that didn't strictly follow the organization's mandates, because that was what resulted in them getting the most funding and freedom to do their jobs in those cases where they were necessary. People like me started being hired on, not to be agents, but to handle the bureaucracy so agents didn't have to. We took jobs in Parks and Rec so that we could go to the agents," Miss Lasko grinned a bit. "And evidence of conspiracy to enforce the law became harder and harder to find."

Mina mirrored the slight grin at the last part, finally relaxing back in her chair a little.

"Your grandfather was pretty famous in certain circles," Deborah said. "Tommy Escalante started out as a delivery boy. Organized crime figures still have flowers at the funerals and weddings. He got very good at just not drawing much attention. For a while, there was a lot of hope that his daughter would go into the real family business ... well, from a lot of people other than your grandfather. He was pretty happy the day she ended up a florist for real."

Mina remembered her grandfather from her youth as a man old before his time, moving around on a cane with difficulty. What happened to his legs was attributed to a car accident, but not the one in which Carmen Escalante, now Cortez, had lost her mother. She recalled her earliest days at the flower shop, before her parents took over fully. They'd been doing a lot of the work for some time anyway. Her increasingly immobile grandfather's real contribution by then was the web of contacts he'd built up. He knew everyone, remembered everyone, had a kind word and a few questions as to health of family or the latest gossip for everyone who came into the shop. As soon as the shop closed, he was much quieter. Closed and private even with family, often citing exhaustion and wanting to just go home to rest, but he'd always be there first the next morning. And now she was hearing him like he was some secret soldier.

"After he got hurt in the line of duty," the Deputy Mayor continued, confirming Mina's most recent suspicion, "he turned the shop into a safehouse. Agents would disappear there for as long as needed, and leave in empty delivery trucks bound for anywhere needed the next time inventory was dropped off. And then there was his registry. There is an amazing amount of history and a whole web of connections between people for the last fifty years in the computers at your shop. It's all in addresses and flower inventories ... but it's still history. You'd be surprised how many cases he got started just with noting who was a whole lot more elaborate with their daughter's wedding or their mother's funeral or their grandson's Chipping Day party than their income would suggest. When your grandfather died, an awful lot of agents were very relieved that he had such a network of friends, so they could safely show up to pay respects. For obvious reasons, most agents don't tend to end up with a lot of close friends."

Mina took all this in, making a mental note to herself to start checking out everything about her grandfather as soon as possible.

"Your grandmother knew," Miss Lasko answered Mina's next question before it was asked. "She was like me. Not part of the organization, but a friend. She worked as a secretary at City Hall for years, keeping track of the political process from near the ground floor."

Mina swallowed. "His accident wasn't an accident. What about hers? She died when my mom was a kid ..."

Chapter Eight

Deborah Lasko sighed slightly. "No one was sure. His cover might have been blown. After that, the shop—in all its functions—and protecting your mother became his only real passions. He poured everything he had into the AIA, and most of the agents old enough to have been there during his tenure were trained under his watch. Most of those have either retired, died, or moved to other cities—thankfully, mostly the latter. Seattle had something of a reputation of excellence among the organization, with how many cases it solved involving Pacific Rim trade and local smuggling through the ports. Everyone wanted agents trained here, rather than recruiting their own." The Deputy Mayor's pride in this fact was not concealed at all.

"And the transfers weren't replaced?" Mina ventured a guess. "You said that the organization was shrinking."

Miss Lasko shrugged. "Changing with the times. The world has moved on. International tensions aren't remotely what they once were. Working together for mutual survival and fighting through growing pains led to something akin to actual cooperation. This century has seen no wars between major nations, just terrorists and isolated violent regimes, neither of which can take advantage of seas of refugees and emergency transfers anymore. Sure, there's always going to be mistrust between uncomfortable bedfellows, but the odds of China and the United States ending up at each other's throats is remote—the current arrangements are too profitable. As the enemies in the world shrink, so too have the forces that the alliance puts out to fight them, and just as importantly, so too does the budget. There are days that fanatical accountants in the halls of power are our

47

worst enemies."

The extremely well-informed civil servant smiled, leaning forward at the desk. "Which is the reason all of you have people like me. You're going to have enough trouble just holding down a full-time job and dealing with your parents, dealing with customers, and dealing with the heavy responsibilities of being part of the invisible line that guards us and our allies. I've already arranged for a new apartment for you through suitable channels. You'll be introduced to your first case tomorrow."

"What is—?"

"I'm afraid I can't give you any details now ... the Director will handle that. Meanwhile, I'm going to give you as many tools as I can to do your job to the best of your ability with as few roadblocks as possible. In the near future we're going to have to keep contact between us discreet, until such time as you're more involved with the Parks & Rec projects, but if you seriously need something, please don't hesitate to contact me, all right?"

"Thank you, Ma'am, I will. I think I should get back to my family though. They'll be worried."

Odd as the afternoon had started, Deborah Lasko and her security detail, the Director, her grandfather, her own chip, her future—a lot of things were starting to make sense. Mina couldn't wait to tell Miko ... that she was a florist. Mina deflated a little, but managed to maintain her smile. Despite feeling just a little less like a proper Mouseketeer, she had to admit, this was a lot more excited than she'd expected to feel at this point after her chipping.

* * * *

Her family, and Miko, had indeed been worried, but they'd been reassured, then put her to bed after her surgical procedure and its minor complications. Mina had barely been able to sleep. A whole new world had suddenly opened up, and she found herself immediately thrust into the middle of it. Worse, she apparently already had a case, and no one was telling her anything. She thought a couple of times about going back to see Director Richter sooner, but her chip and her general fear of the Director told her that was a bad idea. Exhaustion caught up with her enough to get a couple hours of sleep, leaving her bleary-eyed and sleepwalking through the start of her day.

With school behind her, she was up with her parents and off to the shop in the van. Even as tired as she was, the chip practically walked her through the first routines of the day. As long as she didn't fight it, everything went smoothly. Flowers were picked and arranged and put on display, inventory was moved from the back gardening area to the shop refrigeration units, and everything was watered and fertilized in order. By the time the shop actually opened to customers, and the phones were turned on for the day, Mina was waking up, but she barely remembered the morning.

She ran into the first moments of trouble with her weekend work habits. Her shortcuts didn't match the chip's programmed procedures for handling flowers and setting displays. Vague hints of that aluminum taste were followed by burning in her sinuses. Most of the time it was momentary, but she gained a definite feel for when she and her chip weren't in perfect alignment. School had given her a few cases of people with similar sensitivity, especially very early in the process, but not many. A few times she also had to slow down, or was told by her parents to slow down. Outpatient procedure or not, she was still supposed to take it mostly easy, especially after her alleged "complications."

Even so, as soon as the first calls came in for deliveries, Mina couldn't help but launch herself towards the phone. Much as she was aware that the shop was going to be most of her day-to-day life, she couldn't wait to actually begin figuring out precisely how all of this spycraft happened. Her parents were left a little confused by her sudden enthusiasm for the work, but let her take the van out for her first deliveries, to celebrate her first official day on the job full-time, and perhaps they thought she'd strain herself a little less.

If that was what they thought, they were to be disappointed. She ended up making a delivery to the clinic she was told about and was directed downstairs. There, Agent Park was waiting for her. The basement itself had a few high-tech workout machines, as well as an old school treadmill with some sort of suspension device set up over it. Most of the weights were set up over some type of raised plates, partly set into the floors.

"This is where your transformation into a superhuman begins," Agent

Park offered as soon as she laid eyes on the set up, with a wave of his hand. "We're going to take it easy on you today and tomorrow while you adapt to your chip. You shouldn't be jarring it too much 'til everything heals entirely. Still, we can get you used to the routine. I'll be here to supervise, at least for now."

He moved her to one of the raised plates, tapping a button. The ground under her feet started to vibrate, causing her to almost lose her balance a couple times before she found her equilibrium. Then he guided her through stretches while still on the plate. "Everything here is designed to create the most efficient workout possible. You have two types of muscles: slow-twitch and fast-twitch. The first get used for endurance; the second get used for sprinting and bursts of activity. We're building up both at the same time, but especially the fast-twitch."

Mina listened while going through the warm-ups, trying to keep her balance. "So working on these muscles will get my body closer to catching up with my chip's processing speed for physical information?"

"Oh, good. You remember more from that briefing than just 'Director Richter isn't easily interrupted.' That's the goal, yes. You hear stories about how when professional athletes are really on their games, everything slows down for them. When you get adrenaline going, your chip lets you see the world like that full-time. Because we were all on Inquisitor chips, that test-fight would have seemed normal to you, but I suspect it didn't last near as long as you think it did. We'll outdo that."

Mina grinned at mention of the test fight. "Yes, but I hit ... I think that was you, and disarmed agent Hall," she answered.

"Well, yes," he agreed, his own cheerful expression not fading. "That was the idea. When you're a little further from your surgery, we'll try some sparring matches and show you what it looks like when we're not walking you through it."

Mina's grin faded. "I'll be looking forward to it," she answered as any elation from her small victory faded.

From the stretches, she moved onto weights. Squat press, military press, bench, each time on one of the platforms, stressing muscles each time, especially in her calves and thighs that the weightlifting itself didn't bring into play.

"You're going to notice drastic jumps in your weightlifting

maximums, your muscle endurance, and especially your reaction times within a fairly short period. The training regimen you've been under already did wonders for you, or you wouldn't have been a candidate. Now, we're moving you to the type of training you'd be under if you were going into professional sports, except your chip is a lot more complex than any athlete's."

As she lifted weights, Agent Park started telling her stories of his own years as a spy. Despite the fact that, as a personal trainer, he was a sadist, Mina found herself liking the man. He'd seen a lot of cases come and go. Some of the stories weren't even about his Inquisition cases, but just his work as a policeman, then as a detective on the force.

They moved to the treadmill eventually. Expecting to end up jogging or something for an extended time like some of the warm ups she was used to, she was surprised when he helped her into a vest attached to a suspension harness. "If you fall, the machine will catch you. Because you will fall," he told her. "You're right-handed. Stand, facing me, to the side," he instructed, as he turned the treadmill on. He kept increasing the speed of the machine as she shuffled laterally. He helped coach her through proper movement, improving her speed, then dialed the machine up 'til she could no longer keep up.

"Twelve miles per hour ... now ..." he turned the machine off and turned her around, then started the process again. She didn't get up to nearly the same speed before losing her balance.

"Just like you have a dominant hand, you have a dominant leg. You can currently pivot or push off, or maintain balance much better going one direction than the other. We can't have that, so we're going to train that out of you."

A short break followed for water, finally, before they did one more set of exercises on the treadmill. This time, he dialed up the suspension to help hold her more upright and took some of her weight off her feet. "Currently, your legs will only move you so fast. We're going to train the fast twitch muscles to fire faster, partly by making you run in these conditions faster than you currently could if you weren't suspended, at half weight. When those muscles are trained, eventually, your speed will improve and then we'll turn the treadmill up higher." Indeed, he got her up to twenty three miles an hour on the treadmill before she was having to rely entirely on the harness.

Finally, Agent Park called it for the day. He brought her a couple of fruit-and-nut granola bars from the storage unit, along with more water. It was a while before she was feeling up to walking again, but eventually she had to get back.

"You'll have a couple hours at the shop, pending any actual deliveries, then the Director will be calling. Good luck," Agent Park offered, genuinely, on her way out.

At that moment, it wasn't that Mina wasn't looking forward to her introductions to spycraft still—more that all she really wanted was to go home and sleep for about ten hours after this first introduction to her new spy routine. She was especially not looking forward to waking up tomorrow morning, as sore as she already was.

* * * *

Mina received the next set of instructions piecemeal. She got a call for a delivery. As soon as she reached the light rail station, she got a direct comm that her chip picked up as a secure priority message. Instead of her original destination, she was to take the light rail north into the University District. She followed the instructions her chip gave her to interface with her comm, hacking into the system in order to broadcast false coordinates, so if her parents checked in on her, it would tell them she was on her way to the original destination.

As soon as she got off the light rail in the mostly deserted University District, she was given an updated set of directions. She passed the various establishments set up to cater to the academics and archivists still employed with the University of Washington system. Most of the buildings had been converted from larger establishments as recently as fifty years past, when the University was still hosting students, whether because people had opted out of chipping due to health quirks, or further assessments were necessary at a higher level to match the most complex chips to candidates.

With leaps in data storage, and increased ability to update chips, the purposes of the Universities had shifted. Now, the quiet grounds were for people like Dr. Kimura, who were advanced enough in a subject, or in multidisciplinary studies to not simply take their chip and do a job perfectly, but to innovate in their fields. Miko's father ran the second largest pre-Decimation archives on the West coast and published regularly in scholarly journals on topics of life in the 20th and 21st centuries. Plenty of people with the right chip could tell you about the history of car manufacturing in the United States. It took geniuses like Kenichi Kimura to restore 114 year old cars found buried in pre-quake ruins. Mina wasn't quite sure if Dr. Kimura's being able to sing all the top hits of 1983 was quite as useful, but she definitely appreciated Miko having Vlad.

As she passed several open spaces, Mina could imagine them filled with people her age. Now, everything was tailored to people like Dr. Kimura; locations had names that were references to things that flew over Mina's head. All of the buildings of the University itself were similarly tailored to their fields. Looking in windows as she walked revealed rooms structured very similarly to her school classrooms, but now full of books, machinery, historical artifacts, models of star systems or early humans, and various other things she couldn't identify. There were a few people about, but no one took much notice of her.

Mina continued to follow directions which updated themselves every time she thought she might be nearing her destination, before finally heading into one of the buildings near the center of the university. The chipped instructions led to an elevator. Once within, there were a few moments of confusion before Mina rolled with going through rote actions, guided by her chip. She opened the emergency panel, disengaged two wires which were mounted loosely, then touched the tips together. The elevator hummed into motion. The lights showed her going into the basement. Motion continued well past that point, with the elevator doors finally opening some distance beneath the ground. Her instructions updated, leading her down a hallway. Rounding a corner, she almost ran into the Director.

"Miss Cortez," Director Richter said without prelude. "This is Seattle's central chip programming center. There are only four like it in the United States. Aside from your own, and that of a few of the nation's highest officials, the people who work here have some of the highest security clearances available. This is where your own chip was developed. This is also where Scott Szach worked before his disappearance."

Jeffrey Cook

Chapter Nine

The statement took Mina aback. Common sense and her chip quickly informed her that it was highly irregular to put an agent on a case involving someone they were close to. Much as Scott had been on her mind, she hadn't remotely made a connection, partly because this was against proper procedure, partly because she simply hadn't considered that this was the sort of thing the AIA would handle. Of course, now that she was here, it made sense that they would, but not that she'd be called in on it.

The Director led her through two security doors, pushing in a code before both she, then Mina, had to pass fingerprint, eye recognition and voice recognition tests at each station. As they went, the Director talked, sounding like she was not pleased in the least to have Mina there. "This installation was largely protected by anonymity. The programming center was moved here thirty years ago. Black marketeer infiltration into both military ranks and a handful of private security services complicated security for programming and data loading onto highly sensitive chips. Reactionary terrorists also hit the Houston facility around that time, using a targeted EMP pulse to shut down everything, and destroyed a lot of the chips in development. Since then, the data on chips is better protected, though a strong enough pulse will still cause reboot and recovery periods. Everything needed for high level testing was here, but since production continued in Redmond, most people assumed the programming was also done there."

Mina kept quiet, pretty certain that telling the Director that Scott may have mentioned that detail wouldn't help any at this point.

"Despite that, no one trusted a bit of misdirection to hold up, however much appearances were maintained," the Director continued. "This place has state-of-the-art security. This sub-basement doesn't exist on any maps or blueprints. The elevator system shouldn't be obvious to most. Then there's the codes, plus three-step identity verification. If every person in a group doesn't pass each station, the doors won't open, to prevent people from taking a single worker hostage and forcing them to lead through security. Significant security resources are available should a single alarm be triggered. Additionally, every inch of this place is monitored by security cameras at all times."

The second set of doors opened when Mina finished her verification. Just inside the door, they were met by a middle aged man. Only a few inches taller than Mina herself, he was heavyset and looked even thicker due to a full, slightly unkempt beard and thick glasses. He wore rumpled clothing and smelled like he'd been in that same set of clothing for a couple days. Over it all, he wore a taupe gray jacket with ivory lettering on the arms and back reading 'SECURITY', though he didn't look much like any security guard Mina had ever seen. Given the cramped quarters and stale air of the place, she decided she wouldn't mind not seeing him again any time soon.

"Miss Cortez, this is Fulton Hawkins, director of security. Fulton was the one who first reported multiple programmers missing and found the floor supervisor's body."

Mina was certain that Fulton Hawkins had some kind of title he was used to going by, or at least would typically be Mr. Hawkins, Chief Hawkins or Director Hawkins, to those outside the facility. Based on Director Richter's subtle body language, the director didn't think much of Hawkins, and insisting on forgoing any hint of formality was an intimidation technique. She was also sure it was working, given the way the basement troll shied away from her boss. Mina still didn't like her much, but suddenly felt a certain tiny amount of perverse pride at the reaction.

After a couple of moments of uncomfortable staring, Fulton seemed to realize it was his turn to talk. "Normally, all the stations are monitored from the electronic security room. Accessing it requires going through an additional layer of security, with different codes. My security chip syncs with the algorithm it uses to generate the codes," he explained, drawing a quirked brow from Director Richter and an impatient glance from Mina. "That means that I could open the door, but no one else. I can see the whole facility from in there. The cameras shut down, and the doors locked me in. The University is on its own power grid, and we have our own backup down here. That shouldn't have been possible. And had there been any serious interruption, it should have set off an alarm to at least get someone checking things out. We're too far underground for me to call out using my subdermal comm, so I had to wait 'til systems came back up to get out. I couldn't have been stuck in there for more than ten minutes, max. When I got out, the supervisor was dead. Someone had shot him in the head. He was just ..." Fulton gestured. "... just lying over there, face down. No signs of a struggle or anything. All of the programmers who had been on duty were gone. Again, no struggle, no nothing. The cameras caught nothing. No alarms went off, but all records of entries and exits were wiped for a half hour period. Any of the programmers could have pulled off that kind of hack, but not many others. This is high-level stuff. Even they should have set something off if they'd tried to hack it."

He led them around the facility, cramped, kept cool, full of some of the highest-end computers Mina had ever heard of. Basement troll heaven. She could see Scott being very happy in here ... though probably even happier if a couple of the lights had been a bit higher. She was almost positive he'd hit his head a couple times while getting acclimated. As soon as the brief tour, which included the security room, ended, Director Richter thanked him with a distinctly 'you are dismissed now, Fulton,' tone to the politeness. Despite the few options in places to go, he found somewhere to disappear.

"Miss Cortez, you'll be given full access to all of the crime scene photos. Both of the other city agents have been down here and surveyed the scene. There are painfully few people to be interviewed. You just talked to the primary one," she began. "Obviously, Fulton Hawkins remains a suspect, but he's under almost constant monitoring. He's also been here for several years with no hint of any incident. Whatever else he is, Fulton is, historically, honest and good at his job of watching screens and programming security codes. If he had anything to do with this, he's made no contact whatsoever with the hostages."

Mina was already trying to envision the scene, and running through the reactions she could imagine from Scott, and a handful of other people like him, to being kidnapped. Following the directions and locations Hawkins had given them, Mina moved to examine Scott's work station while Director Richter continued.

"All of the computers have been swept for any signs of a clue as to what happened. No one seemed to have left any kind of warning messages or hints. Everything was undamaged and in full working order. The only hint of violence was, obviously, the supervisor's death via a single shot to the back of his head. Going by his expression and posture, he did not appear unduly alarmed. We're fairly certain that he was taken by surprise near the start of the kidnapping. We're also quite certain that this was, at least in part, an inside job. Someone with extensive knowledge of this facility and its systems had to be involved. Even then, we have numerous inconsistencies."

Mina continued to search the workstation, looking for signs her friend had been working here, or what he was working on at the time. While most of the stations had small signs of the personalities and interests of the users, Scott's station was mostly clear aside from a coffee cup and a modified ocular implant interface. Given his home computer station, she was pretty sure he just hadn't had much chance to move any of his toys in yet.

"Additionally, while the University grounds are quiet, a group that size would draw attention. In any direction, a group would have had to pass any number of buildings, and eventually, traffic monitoring cameras to get in and out of the university. No one on campus at the time saw any groups in the area. Authorized security has swept through every building on campus, out to the streets on all sides. We're monitoring every black market contact we're currently aware of for signs of additional chips becoming available, as numerous chips and programs were taken, but not wiped off of the existing computers. Everything was done within a narrow time frame, since the gap in the cameras, as Fulton indicated, is not long."

Mina approached the Director again, talking more quietly now, with one big question remaining on her mind, above and beyond the mysteries presented by this case. She could absolutely see the value both in the programs, and especially the people capable of creating those complex programs. The motivation was simple. The ways to pull off the disappearing act weren't, but obviously those had been under analysis for a while by the AIA

"So ... why me? You could call other agents and specialists in. You have two other agents, and you obviously know the case. I mean, sure, I appreciate knowing what's going on here ... but isn't this kind of a breach of protocol? Scott is my friend. I'd do anything to find his kidnappers, but this is ..."

Director Richter cut her off, narrowing her eyes. "We are pursuing every angle. This is a matter of security on the highest level, and I trust you to act professionally. If I didn't, you wouldn't have gotten that chip, Miss Cortez. However, you misunderstand. Every other programmer here had a significant work record and history with the facility. Mr. Szach was a borderline case. He had a history of system hacking, but his profile indicated that this tendency was benign. Nonetheless, he almost didn't get the assignment. He was the newcomer, and in his first day, received a black mark for a near altercation with his supervisor. When this happened, he was under review and at risk of losing the job right after getting it. At this time, we brought you in on the case due to your familiarity with Scott Szach's habits, because evidence suggests that he is currently our primary suspect."

Chapter Ten

Despite the shock of the news, and her obvious conflicts over it, Mina had been expected to continue her work and go about her day like any other. Throughout much of the day, she was glad for the chip's ability to let her go into near auto-pilot for many tasks without risk of mistakes. Her mind was much more on the data drive in her pocket than the flowers in her hands. She had to keep herself from fidgeting with it as she thought. The drive had the record of Scott's argument with his supervisor, as well as extensive records of his history of hacking the school's systems, along with the service records of the rest of the programmers.

That afternoon, between her two actual flower deliveries, she was given additional information and assignments. Whoever was on the inside had to have help from someone within the black market or some other criminal organization. All of the agents in the city were following up on various leads, and Mina would be no exception. The following day, following training, she was going to be sent into the International District on a fake delivery to look into one of the likely fronts for black marketeers with the resources to move counterfeit skill-chips.

Mina was so lost in that train of thought that she almost missed her mother talking to her near the end of the workday.

"Mina, honey ... it's time to go."

"Wha ... oh? Another delivery?"

"No, honey. Your dad has the van ready. I know you haven't had much chance to pack, but they've already arranged for your new apartment. We thought you might like to take a look at the place and see what you're going to need. Amiko started getting some things together for you to move, so you wouldn't be moving anything too heavy or pushing yourself too hard after the difficulties."

"Oh ... I'll be sure to thank her. I can handle packing. I would like to see it, though," Mina agreed readily enough. That much was true. In addition to just the thought of having her own place, she was liking the thought of having somewhere she didn't have to pretend to have her mind on flowers, deliveries, and landscaping.

"Then get going. Your dad is waiting." Mina's mother hugged her. "Thank you for the hard work around the shop. It's already making a big difference having you here, honey."

The trip to the apartment wasn't a long one. It only made sense, of course, that Mina should be within easy biking distance of the flower shop. All in all, it wasn't a bad place. Modest, certainly, befitting her supposed income. She'd eventually get an upgrade if she got married and combined incomes, or when she took over the business entirely. Until then, this would be her home. The elevator took them to the seventh story, the top floor.

"Seriously, Dad, I can help with stuff. I've been making deliveries all day."

"There's not a lot just yet, sweetie. Just sit down at the window."

Looking out over her little section of West Seattle, she had to wonder if it was intentional that the chipping center recommended a place with such a view. Most of the neighborhood was older-style architecture, some of it dating back over a hundred years, to the reconstruction. Few other buildings in the area were taller than three stories, built in an era when earthquake paranoia was at its height. The building was also at the top of one of the region's many hills, giving Mina a fantastic view in two directions from her corner of the building. Nothing in her chip's knowledge stores indicated she had any particular lookout duties here, so, she figured, it might just be that if they were going to give their highly paid agent a lower-middle-class apartment, they at least gave her one with a view.

Jim Cortez set down the last of what they'd brought. "This was in the blankets," he said as he handed his daughter a note. Mina read it.

Mina,

61

Don't worry; I'll let you handle most of packing your own room, but here's enough to set up your kitchen. There's also some blankets and pillows so you sleep at the apartment, if you want. Also put in the music player in case you need to think. *Some* of us still have school, but Dad will partially let me off practice this weekend for an unpacking sleepover!

Be seeing you,
Miko

After weighing the benefits of personal space against having access to her computer and her own bed, Mina finally assured her father she'd be fine for the night, and would be at work on time the next morning, even setting her chrono's alarm five minutes earlier to make sure she had plenty of time, while he was there, watching. As soon as he left, Mina took a few deep breaths and turned on the music player, trying to help herself relax enough to process everything. She settled in at one windowsill, looking out over the cityscape of her new home.

Somewhere out there was one of her best friends. Her real employer had him at the top of a list of suspects, though far from the only one, at least. Regardless of the truth, he was now either working with or in the hands of someone dangerous enough to have raided the high-end facility. She would be given every chance to help discover the truth of the kidnapping, but even Mina had to admit, the evidence looked quite strong that an inside presence had to have been involved. Her chip helped her run through the logistics, letting her perfectly picture the maps and camera patterns of the area. Every scenario she could easily come up with was impossible to execute within the time frame and data they had.

Mina fidgeted with the drive. Scott currently looked like the strongest case for an inside job, not that she believed that for a second. To clear him, though, she'd still have to follow all of the leads and take advantage of the one thing she had that the other agents didn't—direct familiarity with one of the victims. Even if he wasn't involved with the kidnapping, whoever was almost certainly wanted Scott, and the others, for their knowledge and computer skills. As such, her knowledge might still be valuable in tracking them down if he had any access to systems with internet access, or some way he might be able to plug into something that did.

Despite her best intentions to eventually try to make something of a bed for herself, Mina ended up falling asleep in the windowsill, still trying to find the one detail someone had missed. By the time she drifted off, she was still no closer than when she started.

* * * *

Mina woke with a start. Only her newly chipped reflexes kept her from tumbling out of the window. All the chipping in the world wasn't going to do a thing about the crick in her neck. She took her bike into work, arriving ten minutes before her shift, and promptly reset her chrono alarm to five minutes later. Any hint of smugness didn't last long, before her mother set her to work arranging the display cases.

She'd only just finished with the displays when the phones turned on for the day, and, as she expected, she promptly got calls for three deliveries. As it turned out, use of the van had been a first-day thing, since all the deliveries were in biking range. She made the one legitimate delivery first, then plugged in the code her chip gave her to hack her tracker and falsify her location, then headed for the hidden gym. Agent Park's idea of 'easy' was no kinder than the day before, but at least this time she knew what to expect. What she didn't expect was how quickly the program was taking hold. Even in just her second day, she showed measurable improvement in her top speeds, and especially her balance and greater ability to use her off-hand and off-foot. The progress was almost distracting from her contemplation of the case.

"Not bad, Cortez, but try to keep your mind a little on the exercise."

"Right. Sorry. Scott being a suspect is … just …"

"—a lot to take in for you, yeah," Agent Park said with a sigh. "There's a reason we have policies in place to avoid that sort of thing. Don't take it personally, Mina. I learned about taking cases personally the hard way. One of my former partners—he was a good cop—an actual cop, not an agent. We'd worked together about five years and were pretty close. Jonas was the first time I got to be the one to give the chips-are-a-tool-not-a-crutch speech."

"There's a speech?" Mina said breathlessly as she tried to keep up with the treadmill.

"Only among a few cranky old men. Chips never replace instinct. Especially in our line of work. They're always handy, but if you're the type to get the Inquisitor chip, odds are good you have a good sense for things, and it won't always agree with the chip. Usually I say trust your gut. Programmers are good, but they don't do what we do and can't prepare for everything." He sighed, turning the treadmill off, calling a break while he got back off the tangent.

"So, anyway, I'd been working with Jonas five years. I got to be the cranky old man. He got a little too enthusiastic and got himself hurt, bad. He didn't even see the attacker, but I'd seen the M.O. I'd practically seen the same ruined leg before, on Tommy Escalante."

Mina was still trying to catch her breath. "Abuelo … the same people …?"

"Not the exact people, but a related cartel. I was sure of it. More sure, and more specific about who, the more I looked into the case, and the Inquisition files. But I couldn't prove anything, and trying to would have put the organization at risk. The cops kept me away from the case, and the Inquisition gave me an enforced vacation ... and it was the right call. I don't know what I'd have done without some time in Florida to cool down and get my mind right. We eventually got the guy who crippled Jonas, three years later, on an unrelated case that I wasn't even involved with."

Mina nodded sympathetically, then said, "And you think I ..."

Agent Park put a hand on her shoulder. "If this case wasn't an emergency, they'd have done the same. Recruited you, then had you trained somewhere else. They'd have found a way to cover it with your parents. Putting you on this isn't policy, but even if I disagree, I have to acknowledge that this is about as bad as it gets."

"Really?" Mina asked, trying to get her mind off the personal level.

He nodded. "Sure, there's plenty of black-market chips. Some of the good ones are even pretty sophisticated, but having actual programmers hostage gives them potential to produce things on a new level. Worse, in the short term, those people handle the programming for everything. They can access information on almost every security system on the West Coast, or the inner secrets of the political machine, shipping and travel schedules for everything and everyone going through the region, plus the Inquisition."

Mina blinked. "I hadn't thought of that."

"Yeah. They've had access to data on how we operate, how to identify agents. We have to get this shut down, and fast. Not going to give you much time to learn or grow into the job, I'm afraid."

"Thanks for being honest," Mina replied, sincerely. She still wasn't entirely comfortable with what she was being asked to do, after all. She hesitated a moment, pondering approaches to trying to convince her fellow agent that Scott couldn't possibly be responsible. She'd been brought in, after all, for her direct, applicable knowledge, and that was one thing she was sure she knew. She decided that wouldn't help her case any, nor convince Agent Park that she could handle the unusual assignment after all. "I'll do everything I can to help solve the case," she offered instead.

* * * *

Her next delivery was in the International district. She was still restricted to her bike, since her father had the van out on park business, but the district was readily accessible by biking to the nearest light rail station, and taking it a bit further north. After the intense workout, she was glad for the opportunity to coast down the steep hills leading from the station down to the shops, while simultaneously dreading the trip back uphill.

This time, it wasn't about training. She was supposed to make a couple of quiet deliveries to shops in the area as anonymous birthday presents and the like, allowing her to closely monitor the traffic around a particular teriyaki and pho restaurant. Mina quietly reported in as soon as she reached the correct block. "I can see Lucky Pho from here. You really think they'd be keeping them at a restaurant, with all those people coming and going?" she asked.

"Not our highest priority watch," the Director answered. Of course it wasn't, Mina thought. They wouldn't put the rookie on those. "But it's still on the list. Delivery trucks and large groups wouldn't draw attention. They shouldn't have a basement, but the area reports suggest that it was built on top of the older international district—a lot of which was quakeproofed enough to still be stable if someone dug down to it."

"Okay, so supplies and potential places to hide people. What else put them on your list, exactly?"

"This is part of a longer-term operation, Agent Cortez. At least one of the Lucky Pho partners definitely has a hand in some of the smuggling through the ports. We want to figure out whom he's working with but haven't been able to get too close."

Mina nodded unnecessarily. Apparently, the AIA checked in periodically on several similar suspicious places all around the city. At such times as they had enough proof on site, or they tracked down one of the higher ups through their surveillance, then they'd get the FBI, local law enforcement, or someone else involved to actually conduct a raid. AIA agents themselves almost never got directly involved, except as part of their day jobs. "Haven't been able to get close to a restaurant?"

"Not in any meaningful way. We know the food is terrible, the service is worse. They seem to actively discourage too many customers, and yet remain open year after year. The story on their taxes is that they keep getting bailed out by rich relatives. We just wanted to figure out who, precisely, this rich uncle is."

"Understood. So no stopping in for lunch between deliveries. Got it." She could hear the Director's exasperated sigh. Apparently she didn't take much to the efforts to lighten the tone. Mina elected not to push her luck any further. "Anything else I should be looking for?"

"We're pretty sure they're running protection rackets through the area. Small-time stuff, trying to earn a little money on the side. If you see them out and about taking up a collection, don't let them get a good look at you. You're there on legitimate business, but we'd rather you not be seen at all, especially close to any of their operations."

"Understood. Starting to move now."

Mina went on comm silence. The Director could check her locations if she wanted to, but otherwise, Mina was on her own doing Inquisition work for the first time. The district was busy. Small import shops, groceries, and Asian-language vid-and-file stores lined the way along with a variety of restaurants. There were plenty of other people on bicycles, along with plenty of wandering college students, so Mina blended in relatively easily. She took her time about the first delivery, weaving through people to buy herself more time to keep an eye on Lucky Pho.

She took the elevator for one of the post-Decimation-era foot bridges spanning the street, then paused midway across. There were plenty of others climbing the bridge's steps, admiring the scenery, and reading historic placards.

The only thing she was able to notice from higher up that she hadn't seen from below was a delivery truck pulling up to the back. There were no signs of the truck opening or being unloaded, though three people from inside did come out, and engaged the driver in conversation. Eventually, she left the bridge and continued with her delivery. The first was made easily enough. An older woman at one of the groceries received anonymous birthday flowers. Mina slipped back out post-delivery as the woman and the other store employees nearby started speculating.

Moving across the street, she passed by Lucky Pho's spacious—and mostly empty—storefront. She did note a few employees moving about inside, but no actual customers. The place was amazingly well staffed for a place without much business. As she passed by the next alley, she noted the delivery truck she'd seen moving slowly down the back alleyway. At the next footbridge, a few blocks later, she went back up, scanning past the low buildings as best she could until she found the delivery truck again, this time parked behind one of the other stores along the street. Once again, no sign of any deliveries being made.

Mina crossed the bridge, moving towards her second delivery. Had she not been looking back towards Lucky on a regular basis, she'd have missed them. Three men, dressed similarly to the people she'd seen talking to the delivery driver. She couldn't tell if they were the same, as she'd been too far away before, but guessed they likely were. Her chip quickly drew her attention to small details that didn't fit right. While each wore similar light jackets, the sleeves weren't quite long enough to entirely conceal hints of tattoos that reached to the wrists on two of them. She also picked up signs off of each that they were armed: well concealed guns, but guns, nonetheless. Remembering the earlier warning, she made sure not to stare too long, while still keeping track of their progress.

The three stopped at a few stores along the way, not too far behind Mina, emerging each time and heading further down the street. She lost sight of them amidst making her second delivery, this time dropping off congratulatory 'Just Chipped!' flowers at a vid-and-file shop. She didn't have quite the same chance to quickly slip out this time, as the recipient's mother had to call her from the stockroom to come get the bouquet herself.

Mina and the Chinese girl spent a few moments explaining to her parents that they weren't schoolmates, and no, the flowers weren't from Mina; she was just the delivery girl. Further assurances she had no idea who they were from, but, yes, she was very happy for the family. She turned down the offer of tea, insisting she had to be going. It was just enough of a delay that she nearly bumped into the three men from Lucky, on their way into the shop, as she was heading out. Noting them at the door, she instead quickly ducked back behind one of the shelf units. She turned her delivery jacket inside out. It would look odd, but the lining was a different color and didn't have the Emerald City logo on it. Then she pulled her hood up and tried to keep her head down.

That was all she had time for before the shouting started. She tasted aluminum as her chip started translating for her, with everyone else speaking rapid-fire Mandarin. The woman who had been at the till insisted they didn't have enough money. The oldest of the three men started threatening her. When that didn't change her insistence that they would give the men everything they had, but it wouldn't be enough, his tone changed as well.

Mina was still in her hiding spot, unable to see, but hearing everything.

There was a scream, and the sound of a gun cocking, then another.

Chapter Eleven

Peeking around the edge, she saw the youngest of the three men grab the teenage girl. The one who would have been safe in the stockroom had Mina not brought flowers, she reminded herself.

A stronger taste of aluminum and hint of burning in her sinuses told her to stay still and out of the way. She ignored it. This was her fault, and worse, people's lives were in danger. She assessed the situation from her hiding spot, peeking around the corner. Two had their guns out, one pointed at the girl, the other with a pistol held up, simply demonstrating its presence. The last had his hand under his jacket, but hadn't drawn yet. Two of the people in the shop only had to drop or dive to have cover, but the girl was out in the open.

Mina moved around the shelving unit to get close to the one with his gun on the girl while he argued with the woman. When she felt she was close enough, she grabbed one of the display cases and tossed it out on the floor.

Hearing the noise, the man spun. He got halfway through demanding to know who was there when Mina burst into motion. Before his finger could squeeze the trigger, Mina got to his wrist. She applied a wrist lock even as she lifted his arm up and away. His finger squeezed reflexively, sending a bullet whining past her ear. He never got off a second shot before she dislocated his wrist with a twist, then disarmed him with her other hand, breaking his thumb and pulling the gun away. Releasing her grip, she finished him with a quick pistol whipping with his own gun.

Before he'd hit the floor, she was on to the next. This one didn't even get a shot off before she'd taken the two steps to reach him and brought an open hand up under his chin in a perfect sapping blow. As he was losing consciousness, Mina shoved him towards the third, directing his fall to occupy the last assailant. She got to that one before he could get his pistol entirely out, catching hold of his wrist. A quick impulse ran her through the basics of the stance he was starting to shift into. She wasn't sure what style of kung fu he knew yet, but she was sure he had training. Keeping his hand trapped in his jacket with one hand, she kicked at the inside of his ankle, rolling it, putting him off balance. As he started to stumble, Mina directed it, her free hand grabbing the hair at the back of his head and slamming his head down on the corner of the wooden vid-store counter.

Without thinking about it, she took all of the guns, wiped her prints off, and set them on the counter. That was the point she realized there were four shop employees looking at her, stunned.

"Call the police," she instructed firmly. As she was doing that, she heard a buzzing from the oldest man's wrist. A few moments later, there was another voice asking what was holding them up. She repeated her instructions one more time, then followed a hunch. She left the store, and its bewildered owners, and grabbed her bike. Then she headed towards the back alley.

Two buildings down, she spotted the delivery driver, holding up his own wrist near his mouth. He obviously still received no response. With a paranoid glance around, he noticed Mina, then yanked the truck door open and jumped in. The engine was still running, and he quickly tore off down the alley.

Cursing herself, Mina took off after the truck. She could still feel the burning sensation in her sinuses, but the chip still let her call up all of her new knowledge of street maps. She was pretty sure by now that the delivery truck was the failsafe measure for the people running the protection scheme. If something went wrong, duck down one alley, and they disappear into a truck just making its rounds. She'd already drawn too much attention, but hoped if all the thugs could be brought in on other charges, the director or Agent Park could at least have an excuse to interrogate them about what was going on at Lucky.

She quickly reasoned that he would be headed for the freeway. It would allow him to put some distance between himself and pursuit. The local streets had too many people wandering and would require frequent stops. She didn't think she'd be able to catch up to the truck directly, but she might be able to cut it off if she could guess its route correctly. Figuring out his most direct route to an exit, she turned down an alleyway, taking shortcuts on her bike that a larger vehicle couldn't.

Pedaling as fast as she could, she used every alley and quiet side street she could to allow her to not need to slow down. She crossed streets far away from crosswalks and lights with their monitor cameras, and headed down her best-guess intercept route. She saw the truck coming as she emerged back into heavier traffic zones, nearing the on ramp. With her bike, she couldn't cut through heavy traffic to get to him, and knew if he reached the freeway, she would lose him so she headed for the stairs of the last foot-bridge he'd have to pass under.

People jumped out of her way as she biked up the steep stairway. Reaching the top, she could just see the truck reaching the bridge. With no time to stop and assess, she let her chip handle all of the speed calculations and headed for the side of the bridge. Pedaling hard as she could to get up to speed, she pulled her feet off the pedals, stood up on her bicycle seat like some kind of stunt rider, and let her front wheel crash into the railing. The impact catapulted her off her bike and over the edge. She hit the top of the delivery truck, and immediately started rolling backwards to break her fall. The truck's momentum, combined with the instinctive breakfall, almost caused her to go falling off the back of the truck, but she managed, at the last second, to fall forward, finding a few points where metal met metal as finger-and-toe-holds.

The truck picked up speed from the ramp, making forward movement difficult. Still, she managed to find enough hand and footholds to pull herself along. She had to adjust again to keep herself from going careening off the side when the truck merged onto the freeway. Car horns blared as people tried warning the driver someone was on his truck. She did her best to stay out of his mirrors, inwardly cursing the helpfulness of the average driver.

She finally pulled herself to the front edge of the cargo container, near the cab on the passenger's side. She was almost out of breath, her arms and fingers ached, but she found enough adrenaline for one more burst of quick movement. She pulled herself forward and over the edge, managing to grab the mirror and get a hand inside the open passenger window, while her feet found the thin running board. The driver startled, turning her way.

As he did, whether out of intent or simply reaction, the truck veered off the road and towards the metal roadside barrier. Mina pulled herself up and through the window just in time to keep her legs from being crushed as metal met metal.

The driver started to pull left, away from the barrier. Not wanting him back out in traffic, Mina grabbed the wheel with one hand and yanked it right, keeping them skidding along the barrier. While fighting for control of the wheel, she found the parking brake and yanked on it. With a horrendous grinding, the truck jerked, throwing both of them forward. Mina managed to stay low, crashing against the dashboard, then under it. The driver wasn't as fortunate, and his chest hit the steering wheel. As the truck skidded to a halt, Mina punched the man once under the jaw, sapping any remaining consciousness. Guided by her chip, she quickly policed the scene. Everything she'd touched was wiped, and her hands were pulled up into her delivery jacket sleeves. As other cars were stopping for a look, she pulled her arching body out of the passenger side window, hit the ground, and let herself roll into the shallow ditch. She took advantage of the spectacle of a car wreck to draw attention away from herself, heading the opposite way of most people. Her current colors had been seen clinging to the side of a truck. Using a couple larger cars for cover, she righted her jacket, fixed her hair, and tried to move without too obvious of a limp.

She could hear the police sirens approaching, which brought a new idea to mind. She called Agent Park, instead of the director. She advised him on what had just happened, without going into too many details. She figured he could make sure the driver was taken into custody, for reckless driving, if nothing else, and that he'd eventually be tied to the other people from Lucky. He wasn't happy with the attention she'd brought on herself in what was supposed to be covert duty, but he quickly set about doing his job.

She turned off her comm and started the long walk back to the bridge, hoping her bike would still be in the area. Her comm soon after started signaling she had a call from the director. Agent Park was doing his job. Mina, meanwhile, on her first day solo on the job, had just managed to do pretty much exactly everything she wasn't supposed to.

She wasn't looking forward to taking this call.

Chapter Twelve

Mina's parents weren't happy about her bike accident, but at least they bought that as a story for why she was sore and bruised. They gave her the rest of the day off, reluctantly. As soon as she was away from the shop, she falsified her location so she'd appear to be heading to her apartment, then headed downtown. The Director was waiting for her, looking none too happy.

The woman didn't need to say a word for Mina to look down sheepishly as she stood across the desk.

"Agent Cortez, I was hoping it was going to be a very long time before we met face to face again. Having to call agents in here too often is frowned upon. However, I thought that perhaps a comm wouldn't get across the gravity of the situation."

"I'm very sorry, Director. I didn't mean ..."

"I'm sure you didn't. I believe your express orders were to not draw attention to yourself. Were they not?" the Director interrupted.

"Yes Ma'am, but ..."

"What part of leaving three armed men unconscious, before chasing down a delivery truck on the freeway, is inconspicuous? Please explain."

"I ... I ..."Mina started, before collecting herself. "There were lives in danger. Some of them were my fault. I didn't chase them down ... they, well, they drew their guns in the place I was delivering to."

"Yes, that's what the reports say," the Director said. "Do go on."

"The guy with the truck ... he was one of them."

"And this vaunted sense of responsibility could not settle for stopping the shakedown, once lives were no longer directly endangered? Besides, of course by you?"

"I—!"

"Oh, of course, I'm sure no additional bystanders were put at risk by causing a highway accident," the Director continued over Mina's attempted protest, her voice dry. "It was impossible to let the truck go? Or call it in?"

"What should I have called it in on, Ma'am?" Mina asked, finding her voice. "I didn't see the license plate. I was too far away, and none of our people were anywhere close."

"Well, perhaps you could have reported the situation to someone who remembered what your job was," the Director said. "Was it worth ruining years worth of investigations into the shop in order to thoroughly stop one hold-up? The first part might have just made them shut down that part of their operation for a bit. Succeeding at a car chase from a bicycle, however, has made certain they'll shut down operations there entirely. Worse, whoever they were reporting to will be a lot more paranoid now. But at least you caught a single two-bit thug." The words were almost individually bit off.

Mina flushed at that. She hadn't meant to mess up the investigation. She still couldn't bring herself to believe she'd done the wrong thing in the first shop, at least, though. "I'm very sorry. I won't ..."

"You won't be doing much of anything for a while except training and consulting, Agent Cortez. You're off of active surveillance for the time being."

"So I'm ... still an agent?" Mina began, a little startled.

"The FBI is screaming over a botched sting, without having a clue where it went wrong. Lucky Pho has been investigated thoroughly ... the police found enough contraband to arrest everyone on site. There are numerous reports of a horrible bicycle accident off a bridge, but no one seems quite certain what happened. Your bicycle was stolen ... which is actually much easier. The pink and green bicycle somewhat stands out, especially while being ridden by a teen male."

Mina bit her tongue to prevent herself from mentioning that the bicycle was lilac and emerald. This was not the time.

Fiona Richter continued. "Bicycle thieves are far less credible than witnesses turning a crashed bicycle in. You otherwise covered your tracks

75

reasonably well. Agent Park is handling a lot of the rest of the covering up for you. You also did quite possibly save four lives, and while you didn't help catch the big fish we wanted, one safehouse for the black market has been shut down, so it's not nothing."

She fixed Mina with a stern glance. "This is, in no way, a 'good job', Agent Cortez. This is not the gold star that covers up massive professional, and literal, damage. These are a few mitigating circumstances. Most important among them is what we did not find. There was no sign whatsoever of any of the programmers. We're still waiting for proper circumstances to allow an interrogation of the captured men, but we've found absolutely no sign any of them have the first clue about the case you're on. There are a lot of very upset people right now, Agent Cortez. You ruined years worth of work, made many people's jobs much harder, and have put me and your fellow agents in a difficult position. However, you're still an agent ... but you now have an official reprimand on your record, and I don't want to hear about any further incidents of this nature. Is that clear?"

Mina nodded quickly. "Yes, Ma'am."

"Good ... then go home and rest up. I suspect you're going to need it. Agent Park is working very hard to clear up your trail within the police department, and I suspect your training tomorrow isn't going to be any fun."

* * * *

The Director had been right. Training wasn't any fun. Unlike the Director, Agent Park didn't scold her. Mostly, he just gave her the exercises and reps, and otherwise didn't say a word. Even when she apologized, he just nodded quietly. In a lot of ways, it had been worse than the verbal dressing down. She suspected for a while that the workout had been dialed up a little more than she'd have thought, but eventually figured it was probably because she was still sore. Agent Park would have followed the book, like every other agent but herself, apparently.

The lack of conversation did mean she didn't end up staying quite as long. After the exercises and a brief water break, she was ready to be on her way. Agent Park did offer a brief "See you tomorrow." But that was it. Under the circumstances, she couldn't entirely blame him. She could only hope things would be a little more relaxed the next day, as she was finding she really didn't want to disappoint her mentor, or come up short of her grandfather's legacy. Amidst the exhaustion, she even spared a few thoughts for not wanting to look bad this early in any records that Agent Hall might see.

With some extra time before her parents would be expecting her back, Mina decided to find somewhere to sit down and have a quiet lunch, instead of one of the rushed affairs back at the shop. That thought lingered a bit, turning into a broader idea. If someone was holding a bunch of programmers, those people would still need to eat. She started using the chipped data to pull up recollections of maps and shops in different areas. At first, the train of thought was overwhelming. There were a lot of places that served food very cheaply. Then a memory hit her.

"Cheap is all very well," Scott had said. "Fast food is one of the wonders of civilization. But it's not just about taste, and not just about affordability, but productivity."

"And that's why you made a graph?" Mina had asked drily.

"That's why," Scott had replied, unembarrassed. "Got most of the major work-food contenders. Axes are 'Easy' and 'Clean.' Pizza's in quadrant four, because hey, it's simple, but I am not getting grease on my machine. But in quadrant one is that great innovation of the legendary Earl of Sandwich."

At this time of day, whoever had them would want the programmers working. They might even let Scott or someone like-minded choose the food options while they did. So sandwiches she would go with. Whoever it was wouldn't risk delivery. Someone might see too much, wherever it was.

It was a long shot, but after her colossal mistakes before, Mina desperately wanted to do something to help put the case back on the right track, and reassure herself she could handle detective work. She found all the sandwich shops she felt she could safely hit and still make it back to work within fifteen minutes of when she was expected back. While she had originally intended to sit and eat, she gave up the idea in favor of her investigation.

The first four had the typical traffic she would have expected in the pre-lunch hours. The fifth was only a little busier. She was about to leave when something about one of the vehicles in the lot made her pause. The car was a nicer model than most of those parked at the various shops, particularly this one. The shop was near two middle-class schools, giving it a regular customer base of teenagers with inexpensive cars. That alone merited only a cursory glance, but that glance picked up on the University parking pass. There were plenty of food options closer to the University, though she supposed it might be someone with only occasional need to stop there.

Nevertheless bothered by this, she decided to go inside and see if anything else stood out. On entering, three people stood out. While most of the few people inside looked like high school students away from campus for lunch, she quickly matched the three older, well dressed men near the counter with the car. Blending in as best she could with the handful of other people her age, she made her way closer to the counter. The person currently at the counter finished his order, with the three men next. As she got close enough, she picked up the odor of gun oil, and hints of cheap cologne amidst the various body washes, soaps, and overloads of perfumes common among some students.

Mina listened as they placed a large order, two dozen sandwiches in all, one of them reading off a list, some of the orders being very specific. The one that caught her attention was the turkey & Havarti, no tomatoes, extra pickles and olives. Scott's usual. She couldn't control a small sound of surprise. One of the men turned, and she caught the sight of his hand darting under his jacket as a reflex to being surprised. She ducked her head down a bit and turned for the door, trying to disappear amidst the few little knots of other students. While she thought they'd missed seeing her face, there was still some commotion behind her.

Chapter Thirteen

Mina darted for the door and then the bike rack, hearing yells and protests behind her. A glance back told her that two of the men were still trying to work their way through people, but one of them was right behind her—the man who'd gone for something under his coat. She was grateful to see he'd thought better of drawing a gun in a shop and drawing more attention to himself, but a quick assessment told her that he'd reach her before she'd be able to get her bike off the rack and get out of the lot.

She pulled her bike free as she reached it, then whirled, trying to catch him off guard. To her surprise, as quickly as she was moving—and much as she thought she'd read him right—he blocked her swing perfectly. His left hand came in low before she could recover herself, knocking the wind out of her. She went into a more defensive stance, and tried to feint to open him up for a return shot, her chip feeding her information and moves as fast as she could process them. He ignored the feint and once again blocked her swing, catching her wrist mid-punch and pulling her into a swing of his own. Mina saw stars as she hit the ground.

"Hey!" came a shout from the parking lot. "Leave her alone!"

Two boys around her age had been leaning against an old beater car, eating their lunch between classes, and had finally caught up with what was going on enough to react. Mina saw the man again go for his gun by reflex, think better of it, and turn to face them. She could see the other two men reaching the doorway, even as the restaurant was exploding into chaos.

Mina kicked as hard as she could for the man's ankle while he was distracted, and he went down hard with a yell. She kicked up to her feet, grabbing for her bike. Out of her peripheral vision, she saw one of the other men who'd been in the restaurant going for a gun, before the last punched his shoulder, shouting something about not being an idiot.

Jumping on her bike, Mina spared a glance back over her shoulder as she headed for the nearest alleyway that went through to the next street, trying to make sure she could disappear before a car could catch up with her. All three had given up on their sandwich order and were running for their car, shoving students out of the way as necessary and keeping their heads down.

It was only when she was several blocks away with no signs of pursuit that she relaxed. As soon as she did, the realization struck her. She'd had to get close enough to pick up the hints of gun oil. Her chip hadn't told her the men were armed. The man who almost caught her—it had read his training, stance, and moves entirely wrong. Worse, he'd moved every bit as fast as she could, countering her perfectly. Something was horribly wrong.

* * * *

After the encounter at the sandwich shop, Mina was positive the three men had something to do with the abduction, and the evidence suggested Scott was still alive. Or someone had the same tastes and allergies he did. As soon as she felt like she had definitely eluded any pursuit, she called the Director. The fact she hadn't entirely caught her breath yet didn't help matters any as she tried to explain what had happened. After forcing herself to slow down, she started over.

"Yes, this is Mina ... I have ... have information."

I'm aware of that, Miss Cortez. I know your number and voice, but you shouldn't be calling here."

"Unless it's an emergency, yes, I know. This qualifies."

There was a brief pause on the other end, and the Director's voice went from mildly scolding to serious. "Are you in some kind of trouble ... again?"

"No ... yes ... I mean ... not immediately. I found something ... someone ... *someones*. I have a license plate number." Mina stumbled over her words, not at all appreciating having the recent events brought up when she was trying to relay critical information.

"What have you done? And what's this about a license plate?"

Mina relayed the numbers and letters. "You need to trace that. It has something to do with the case."

"I'll determine that when you tell me why you think that."

Mina kicked a wall in frustration, but went through the sequence of events. She emphasized how they'd been moving and reacting as quickly as she was, and she hadn't picked up on their being armed until she got close. To her further annoyance, the first thing that got a verbal reaction was when she was asked to explain the bit with the sandwiches again.

After the explanation, the Director began again. "So you got their attention, because they ordered a turkey sandwich?"

"With no tomatoes, extra pickles and olives, yes. And Havarti, not Swiss or Cheddar. You have to specifically order that," she explained, a bit lamely, she felt.

"So you're suggesting that Mr. Szach is in good enough with the kidnappers that he's getting special orders?"

"No, no ... he's ... he's allergic to tomatoes. So it has to—"

"There's a bit more to it than that," came the interruption. Mina, amidst her frustration, was struck by the irony that Director Richter would use that particular phrase, however correctly, when she was the one skipping from criticism to criticism, first implying the sandwiches weren't worth gasping over, then using them against Scott, instead of acknowledging the seriousness of the attackers or researching their vehicle, since they clearly were important.

"Yes, but ... all of the sandwiches ..."

"I got that. Still highly peculiar for a kidnapping, don't you think?"

Mina wanted to scream that that wasn't what was important here, and to forget the damned sandwiches, but felt a few pangs of doubt herself. That was an odd detail, she had to admit, in retrospect. "I suppose, but there's more going on here."

"Yes, clearly someone has chips that at least partially cancel yours out. So they've already gotten something out of the programmers, and seem well aware of us. Did they get a good look at you?"

"I ... I'm pretty sure they didn't. There were a lot of taller people around, all about my age. Even the fight was only a few seconds. They might know these clothes, but—"

She was cut off. "Then you'd best go get changed. I thought I told you to keep your head down, and that you weren't to be involved in the active investigation until further notice?"

"I was just ...?"

"Just investigating, and put yourself in a great deal of danger in the process. I mean it, Miss Cortez. Head down. You're off duty for the weekend. Get your apartment in order, or whatever you're going to do. We'll look into the car."

Amidst the scolding, Mina wasn't sure how sincere the Director was being, or how seriously she was being taken in general, but at this point, the Director's tone told her that was the best she was going to get. "Yes, Ma'am."

Mina was able to describe the three men, but just as she was pretty sure they hadn't gotten a good look at her, most of her details were vague. She knew what kind of clothing they were wearing, their hair colors and rough ages, and that they had on cheap cologne, but she wasn't sure what type. All in all, even to her, it didn't sound like nearly as much as she had thought she had. "Thank you, Ma'am. Yes, I hope there's something useful there, yes," she finished before Director Richter hung up.

* * * *

As soon as the Director had hung up, Mina pondered her options. She would have to get back to the shop and back to work soon. Her stomach still hurt, and she was pretty sure she'd be bruised from the fight, but felt she could manage work. What bothered her more was the implications of the people who moved as fast as she did, and perfectly countered the moves her agent chip gave her.

Above and beyond even that, she was suddenly not at all certain of the Director. They'd brought her in on all of this for some kind of insight, and now that she'd given it to them, it had seemingly been dismissed, or worse, used as further proof of the Director's pet theory.

The situation and lack of sympathy brought Deborah Lasko's offer to mind. Where Mina was hitting a brick wall, maybe the AIA's liaison could do something. She was pretty sure the Director wouldn't be pleased if she knew Mina was calling Miss Lasko, but until she'd done everything she could to make headway in the case, she couldn't give up. Mina dialed the number, which rang several times. As she was about to give up, a familiar voice answered.

"This is the Deputy Mayor's office, Deborah Lasko speaking."

"Miss Lasko, it's Mina ..."

"Mina! Deborah, please. How can I help you? You sound out of breath. Are you all right?"

"I'm fine Miss ... err, Deborah. Or I will be. I've run into some trouble, and just want to make sure that someone is following up. You have ties with the police, right?"

"I do, but it would seem like your Director would be a better call to be making."

"I did call her, but we're not on the best of terms right now. You may have heard—I kind of screwed up my first solo day on the job."

"I heard a little bit, but I also heard something about a delivery girl being credited with saving a few lives. The Director may like things by the book, but the AIA was founded to protect people, after all. You did that."

"I appreciate it, but that's not the important part right now. I have something that I think pertains to the case, and I'm not sure the Director is listening. I want to make sure someone is following all the leads, even if they come from the rookie in hot water."

"Of course, Mina. Tell me what you've got, and I'll see if I can't pull a few strings for you."

Mina gave her the details of the encounter, including the fact her chip hadn't given her the warning she'd have expected. She placed extra emphasis on having the license plate looked into.

"Of course," came the assurance, with more than a bit of surprise in her tone. "Just as importantly, are you all right? Do you need to get the afternoon off so you can rest? Or to get to a safehouse for a little bit? Or medical attention?"

"I'm fine, Deborah, really. I really need to not miss more time at work, and I'm pretty sure it's all just some scrapes and bruises. I also really need to not get any more on the Director's bad side."

"Of course. If you change your mind, I'll make arrangements."

"Thank you, but I really just want to finish up the afternoon and get home."

"Certainly. I'll start having the car looked into as soon as we're off the phone. Don't push yourself too hard, Mina. I know that's difficult advice right now, but we're already short-handed for the situation, and need every possible agent at their best."

"I'll try, thank you, ma—Deborah. I really appreciate it."

"Of course. That's what I'm here for. I'll be looking forward to hearing how your insights broke the case wide open soon."

* * * *

Mina managed to hide her couple of scrapes and not make the tenderness of her side too obvious while finishing work. The couple of times her mother asked about her wincing when reaching for things on higher shelves, Mina claimed lingering effects of her previous accident. Throughout the day, she kept looking towards the front door for some sign that she'd been followed or figured out, but nothing unusual happened.

Miko showed up as soon as the work day ended to help Mina pick up more of her things to take to the apartment. Between the pair of them, they quickly filled up Vlad's back seat and trunk, even with Mina frequently looking over her shoulder.

"Looking for something?" Miko asked.

"Just been a bit twitchy since the bike accident."

Miko continued to look at her a bit suspiciously. "Best friend sense tingling, but whatever."

"I'm not even going to ask how tingling is involved."

Miko sighed. "Culture is dead."

* * * *

Mina began to relax after the last trip through the apartment. It had a solid security system, one of those things her employer apparently checked on when requesting housing for new agents, and Miko's presence was reassuring. She felt a little guilty, considering the circumstances, for not suggesting Miko go home. Nonetheless, she felt more secure and needed the company.

The girls unpacked most of the kitchen supplies and enough extra bedding that Miko could make herself a comfortable place on the couch, once she'd called her father to check in.

"Dad's fine. Wants me home in time for M. Chiasson tomorrow."

"Great ... wait, is that your violin teacher or your French tutor?"

"Both. Real convenient. Three solid hours of mixed lessons with him before krav maga."

The pair stayed up later than Mina typically would have on her own, catching up. Mina continued to feel guilty leaving out some pretty important information, but a lot of it was obviously a necessity. The rote explanation of how she'd managed to get into her bike accident didn't seem to fool Miko either, but Mina eventually distracted her by pretending a renewed interest in some of Miko's old movies. She found herself even able to offer some insight into a couple of Miko's favorite mysteries, even if she had no idea what the weird accent was about or why Miko was calling her 'Sweetheart,' just putting it down to more things she'd never care to spend the hours in front of Miko's antique vid player to figure out.

Miko was just settling in on the couch, with Mina preparing to go to bed, when they heard a noise at the door. Mina quickly hushed her friend, shaking her head at Miko's inquisitive look. She started forward, expecting someone just having the wrong apartment after coming home drunk, but as soon as she neared the door, it started to open, and she picked up cologne and gun oil in strong contrast to the incense she'd been burning while talking to Miko. No alarms had gone off, and it was seconds between hearing the rattling and the click of the lock. Had she been in bed, as she normally would have been at this hour, she'd never have heard a thing.

A hand came through the open door first, with a silenced pistol in it. Mina dove for the door, trying to slam it shut. Instead, she caught the hand in the doorway, resulting in the gun going off, a scream from outside, and the gun falling to the floor. Before she was able to shove the door shut, a shoulder barreled into it, sending her sprawling backwards.

By reflex, she was back on her feet and in stance in a second, feinting at her attacker before going into a low kick. The man in dark clothing ignored the feint, stepping away from the kick. He came back at her while she was still regaining her balance. While it took only an instant, he had already kicked the inside of her plant-foot ankle, sending her sprawling again. She faked rolling one way, and went the other, trying to get back to her feet with some room. He didn't buy it, kicking her in the side as she was trying to regain her feet. Between that and a shot of pain shooting up from her ankle as she briefly put weight on it, she was back down in a moment.

She saw him shift, about to kick downward at her throat.

"Freeze."

Mina and her attacker looked back towards the doorway. Miko had recovered the gun and stood pointing it towards the man. Even as she repeated her warning, properly cop-style, the man was moving. Even with the distance between them, the man's reflexes let him get to Miko to knock the gun aside as she was firing. When the man attacked again, she half expected Miko to brush it aside, or try one of her aikido throws, and indeed, she almost did. He caught his balance and reset his feet too fast for her, and slammed a punch into her face before she could adjust her guard.

That was all Mina saw as she half-crawled, half-dove into the kitchenette, divided from the main room by a short bar-style counter. Using the counter to pull herself to her feet, she saw Miko, still on her feet, but bleeding from the nose and off balance, trading quick punches. She was faring better than Mina had, but the guy was just too fast for her, on top of being bigger and stronger, the advantages her martial arts usually let her counteract. It didn't look like it would last a lot longer.

Mina grabbed for a box on the counter, faced the man who'd broken in, and yelled. With one more quick punch, he knocked Miko to the floor and started for Mina. As she started to throw the box at him, one arm came up to block it. She couldn't see his face, due to a ski mask, but could still see his eyes widen in surprise when instead of throwing the box, she held on to it, just letting its contents fly, and dozens of kitchen knives, forks and other assorted silverware flew his way. Caught off guard, with too much cutlery to properly block or dodge, the guy screamed as one knife caught his arm, while a fork stuck into the side of his face through the mask.

Seeing that that wasn't going to stop him, Mina started reaching for another box—one filled with bread and boxes of crackers. While pretty sure that wasn't going to be nearly as effective, as it turned out, it didn't have to be. Miko had managed to get back to her feet, and as the guy was staggering back, reaching for the fork, she grabbed the back of his collar and waist of his black pants, using his own backwards momentum to get him moving fast and hard towards the nearest window.

Mina's brain was processing the movements fast enough that she was worried he was going to recover his balance and counter the move—and they'd both be in trouble—but he hit the window before he recovered. The impact was enough to break the reinforced glass, and his momentum from the throw enough to propel him through it. He screamed again all the way to the ground, and then went quiet and still on impact.

Chapter Fourteen

"No, that was not a burglar," Miko began, looking daggers at Mina. "What's going on?"

"I'll explain, I promise. But we need to get out of here, now," Mina insisted, limping towards the door.

"We need to wait for the police to file a report," Miko countered, but didn't sound as self-assured as usual.

"When that guy doesn't report in, there'll be more. I'm not supposed to tell you anything, but I think I owe you about a dozen now. My bosses will deal with the situation. But we *need* to go. Just please, trust me."

Miko nodded, quickly pulling her clothes on over her pajamas, grabbing her hat, and heading for the door, catching up with Mina and moving to help support her so both could move more quickly.

There were a good number of people moving about the floor now, reacting to the screams. Miko thought quickly, taking advantage of Mina's injury and the traces of blood. Anyone who looked their way got a quick, "burglar—she was hurt. Move, please."

Meanwhile, Mina thought of a few options for ways out, before a thought hit her. She first headed for the security offices on the ground floor. With the commotion on her floor, this level was empty. The guard on duty was slumped forward over the equipment, but nothing looked tampered with. A quick bit of further investigation revealed he'd been shot in the back of the head. He had never turned towards the locked door to his office, which showed no signs of being forced. Mina quickly grabbed the security vid, hoping it might, on review, give her some idea what was going on, even if its being missing would require some explaining later.

That was all the time for delay Mina felt she had. At first, she started towards her bike, before the taste of aluminum cut off that line of thought. Since the guy who broke in clearly hadn't been expecting Miko, they'd be watching Mina's bike if something went wrong, but might not have the parking area covered. She had to assume there weren't too many of them about since large groups here would be conspicuous at this hour. She suspected, in fact, that there were probably three of them around somewhere—or two, with one having gone through the window. With the time to think about it, she decided that the assailant's body type was pretty close to the smallest of the three men at the sandwich shop, though that was hardly conclusive.

Whether he'd had any backup or not, the girls made it to Vlad, and were able to pull out of the lot without trouble. Mina wasn't able to tell what condition the man was in after his fall, given that there was a small crowd gathered around the area where he would have hit. She recognized a few of her neighbors, but didn't otherwise see anyone she recognized, but from a distance, in the dark, that wasn't a surprise.

Once they got a few blocks away, she started explaining. Miko made her slow down and start over half a dozen times, given how rushed all the details were. Finally, she got out enough for Miko to switch to the questions.

"Okay, so ... wait ... you're just pretending to be a flower delivery girl, and you're really some kind of secret-agent-spy-cop?"

"I know it sounds ridiculous, but ... "

"No, no. I know when you're lying. What I meant to say is that is *so* cool! You're like the last person anyone would expect, so it's perfect!"

"Thanks, I think."

"So, now the not-cool bits. They seriously think Scott had something to do with this?"

"I don't know what to think. Given how quickly they tracked me down, and how quick she was to jump on her own conclusions. I ... I sort of think my boss might know more than she's telling me."

"You really think so?"

"Well, when I called to tell her what I'd found, she was way more interested in jumping down my throat than on, you know, the case. She certainly doesn't seem that worried about me. Maybe they think I'm too much trouble, and they're trying to get rid of me?"

"If they wanted to get rid of you, wouldn't they have just called for a flower delivery to put you where they wanted you, instead of, you know, shooting a security guard and breaking in to a secure building?"

"Okay, point. Maybe so ... I still don't trust her. She's so convinced Scott is behind this, and ... well, you know him."

"Yeah, poking around online is one thing. Hacking school records to see if he can ... sure. Not something like this."

"So, I know what you're going to say, but I need to say it. You shouldn't get involved. This is really, really dangerous. I took the job, you didn't."

"Only because they didn't offer ... yet. You know I'm not going anywhere while you're in trouble. Besides, I know how to prove Scott is innocent."

"Wait, what?!"

"Yeah. We can't go to your place, they might be watching. Probably shouldn't go to mine, just in case ... but that's okay. I suspect no one expects a nine-year-old to be the key to this case."

* * * *

On the way to Scott's house, for reasons Miko hadn't entirely explained yet, Miko tried to get more details out of Mina. "So, if you're a spy on an investigation, and have people after you, shouldn't you be—I don't know—calling in or something?"

"Not yet," Mina said, after a few moments of thought. Sure, she probably should, but something wasn't sitting right so far. "Last time I called in, after the thing at the sandwich shop, my boss just chewed me out. I'll call in when I actually have something. I doubt she cares if I get killed at this point. At least then I'd stop screwing up her investigation."

"So, real hardcase, huh?"

"Total. I'm starting to wonder if there's more to it than that."

"Like what?"

"She seems so convinced Scott is responsible for this."

"Which there's no possible way."

"Right, but she won't believe it. It's like she's not even looking at the evidence, she just wants to pin it on him and have it go away or something."

"You really think that?"

"Sounds crazy, right?"

"A little, maybe ... how much do you know about her?"

"Not much. Aside from being one of the scariest people I've ever met."

"Which is always a prime quality in a boss."

"A boss who is going to chew me out even worse when she finds out that I've told all about her top secret organization to a civilian."

"You mean your organization?"

"Maybe ... this might be my third strike or something ... but I'm going to get to the bottom of this and prove Scott had nothing to do with all this first."

"You mean we are."

"I'm going to be in enough trouble just getting you into this this far. I want to hear this grand idea of yours, then get you somewhere safe. You don't even have the Inquisitor chip."

"Uhm, yeah ... because that did you so much good. Anyway, Scott is my friend ... and so are you. I told you once, you're stuck with me til we finish this. Then we'll figure the rest out. Besides, you're a super spy now. You need a Kato."

"I need a what? Or is that a who?"

"We seriously need to catch you up on your history of great sidekicks. Watson, Kato, Tonto ..."

"Uhm, Watson was Holmes, right? And ... I know Robin."

"You have to ask about *Watson*? Seriously? Okay, fine. I'll be Robin, but I'm the first one. And you're not getting me to wear the short pants, even if you ask really nicely."

"There was more than one?"

"Philistine."

"There's no way I'm talking you out of this, is there?"

"Not a chance in hell, Kemosabe."

"Who?"

"Hopeless. Anyway, you're not going to be able to do this with your bike and public transit, and you're not going to find better wheels than Vlad. So, you know, benefits."

"Okay, okay. So if we can't go to my house, or yours, why are we going to Scott's?"

"Because Beth is there."

"We're not telling her about this. No way."

"Not a word about the top secret spy stuff, no. She knows Scott's passwords though."

"First, you're sure? Second ... so?"

"Positive. On the rare occasions he didn't finish homework by the time he got home, he'd let her log in and play her characters on his accounts. She's almost as good a healer as he is. Even with his cheating with the cyber-eye interface."

"I'm not even going to ask. So why do we need his passwords?"

Miko sighed. "Scott is addicted, and we both know it. If he were some kind of evil mastermind, free to do as he wants, he'd be logging in every day."

"You really think so?"

"Addictions are addictions. Tell me I'm wrong."

"Rarely enough that it gets kind of annoying."

"Love you too. In any case, I'm not wrong now."

"The Director will never accept that as proof of anything."

"No, but it's a place to start. Sure, we know Scott didn't do it, but this will erase all doubt, and we can officially start trying to find a different culprit. Besides, maybe there'll be some kind of clue there. Half of his online friends don't know who he really is. Even without any details, maybe there'll be something in his game mail about his boss, or something. You said they were having some kind of problems ... maybe he complained to someone? Not all the details, but, you know, just that his boss is a jerk or ... something."

"It's a stretch, but maybe. We can check. So how're we going to get Beth's attention without waking her parents up?"

"We just go around back. It's Friday night. She'll have snuck out of bed to get on the computer by now."

"You're sure?"

"Completely. I've babysat a few times on Friday nights after Scott got old enough to be dragged along to events full of snobby rich people his parents thought he should know. That's always where I found her."

Moving around the house and looking through the back window into Scott's main computer room revealed the light off, but the tell-tale glow of the computer screen. Miko tapped on the window, until a small face peeked through it. A few moments of silent gestures got the idea across, and Beth went to the back door and unlocked it. "What are you guys doing here?"

"Shhh," Miko replied. "We need to get to Scott's game accounts, can you get us logged in?"

"Sure, but why?"

"Top secret, Munchkin. But if you do, I'll loan you my vid player for the whole weekend, and set it up with any series you want."

"Leverage?" Beth asked. "Not just cartoons?"

"You don't want to watch cartoons?" Mina interjected.

"Cartoons are for little kids ... and Miko," Beth responded, going with her theme of being too old for all sorts of things, while quickly catching herself before Miko could object. "Besides, Eliot is on Leverage. Pow, pow!" she added, punching the air.

Mina was lost, but not surprised that Miko grinned. "Okay, Leverage. All the seasons." She held up the vid player, starting to work with it. "I'm throwing in A-Team too, which is mostly the same, with more Eliot ... except they call that guy B.A. ... and I think it a couple years earlier." A pause in her plugging in chips from her collection. "But only after you get us in."

"Sure!" Beth said, then hushed her voice, glancing towards the hallway. With no sign of stirring, she ran to the computer room followed by Mina and Miko. Logging out of her game and into Scott's took only a few moments. As soon as they were in, Miko took the computer chair, getting quick lessons from Beth on how to navigate around between Scott's various characters and accounts, and determining which were his and which were Beth's. As soon as she felt they had enough, she handed the vid player over to Beth, who quietly headed into the next room, the Szach kids' main TV room, with its own entertainment system and big screen, so they could watch their shows or play video games while their parents used the main living room.

Miko logged into the first character, found nothing there, and moved on. By the third, they had found an apparent main character, or at least one who got a lot of in-game mail. They started going through it, looking for anything out of the ordinary. By the dates on the unread mail, they could be fairly certain Scott hadn't logged into that character. They left much of it unread if it seemed to have recognizable game-related titles so they had some kind of evidence chain, while looking through anything that stood out.

"Still nothing," Miko responded after a few. "But at least now we can be pretty certain he hasn't logged in."

"Not til we check all of his characters," Mina reminded her. "I'd like to just leave it at that, but I need to be thorough on this. While we're on the computer, when we finish this, we should take a look at the security film too. I could play it on something smaller, but you traded away your vid player, and this screen will let us see more detail," she added.

"Good idea," Miko agreed. "We'll do that next. I don't think we're going to find much as far as work stuff here, but we'll keep checking."

They went through the rest of the characters on the account, confirming all of the dates as best they could. Near as they could tell, only Beth's had been logged in at all recently. Not all of the others could be confirmed for certain, but enough could to leave a definite pattern. Nothing regarding work commentary, but much as Miko tended towards optimism, Mina hadn't expected anything to be there. Scott was too paranoid about his own security, and while some of the people online wouldn't know who he was in real life, enough would that any information leaks could get back to him. At best, she figured he'd probably vented about his boss being a jerk a few times in whatever chat they were using. While she was sure Beth knew some of Scott's friends online, she didn't want to start bringing anyone else in on any part of the investigation, witting or not.

She, and probably Miko, were in enough trouble already, and while she hadn't had much choice on Miko getting involved, she otherwise wanted to at least try to be responsible about this after the trouble she'd already gotten into over the two previous incidents. If her boss was somehow involved in some sort of problems, or was trying to make the case go away, that was one thing, but she had nothing but suspicions so far.

After they went through the characters, with Mina taking notes on character names and last confirmed log-in dates, as well as records of previous game activity, as much as they were able to determine that with their limited experience with the game systems, they logged out and put the security vid chip into the computer.

The first thing that really surprised Mina was that the intruder had apparently just walked in from the street. He seemed to have some idea of where the cameras were, and kept his face hidden. Mina couldn't determine anything more about him from the vid that she hadn't already known, but suspected that people had seen him on the street. Presumably that meant the police would have determined his identity, which also meant she might be able to get some information from Agent Park or Hall soon enough.

Agent Park, at least, she still felt like she could trust. She'd need his kind of resources to get much further, but felt he would at least believe her about the account. Following that trail of thought, she felt her first spark of optimism that maybe things could be worked out. She'd taken his advice, and followed her gut. She had made some mistakes, sure, but she was pretty sure that the cop would also want the evidence in the case, and could follow up on some of it ... and maybe give her some tips on dealing with the Director. Maybe he'd even be willing to go with her to speak to the Director, as she was pretty sure that this was going to be another of those situations that merited an in-person briefing. She wasn't looking forward to it, but if they were able to clear Scott, and make some real progress in finding both him and his kidnappers, then she figured that whatever happened to her would ultimately be worth it.

As they were getting to the part of the vid near Mina's apartment, the man had pulled on the ski mask fully. She was able to see bits of the fight through a hallway security camera past the open door. With a little bit of manipulation of the vid, she was able to get a few good looks at the violent exchanges between Miko and the other man.

As she messed with the camera angles, the girls heard a squeak from the doorway. "That's so cool!" Beth exclaimed. "That icon really looks like Miko ... I knew they were getting better at customizations in some of the new games, but hadn't seen anything like that. Can I make a character?"

Chapter Fifteen

"Games?" Mina started, then looked to Miko, and quickly nodded. "Oh yeah, video game."

"We can't really tell anyone we have this," Miko quickly added. "It's a beta test, which is why we needed Scott's system. Our computers wouldn't play it right. No room for any other characters now, since it's just a beta," she replied apologetically.

"That's okay. How do you play? What's it going to be called? And are they going to improve the ninja's A.I. before release? Because, I mean, he's fast, but that's a pretty terrible intelligence. Some of my old little-kid games were better."

"What do you mean?" Mina asked. "And how long have you been watching?"

"Maybe a minute or so," Beth admitted. "I'm sorry. I had to see what was so top secret."

"Okay, okay, but you can't tell anyone or ... or I'm going to replace all of your Leverage and A-Team with Rugrats for the weekend," Miko threatened.

Beth quickly grew wide-eyed and nodded. "Okay, I won't tell anyone."

"Okay, but what's wrong with the A.I.?" Mina repeated, getting back to that, suddenly curious.

"Rewind it, I'll show you. Geez, you'd think they'd pick beta testers with more gaming experience. I mean, I guess the camera angles and stuff might make it hard anyway, and he's really fast ... but if the slower, stronger bad guys are this bad, it'll get too easy for *real* gamers."

As soon as the girls rewound the vid, Beth started pointing out bits of movement. "See, like that. He keeps just getting back into the same position. Every punch and kick is the same angle." she explained. Slow motion going back and forth through the vid confirmed it. Every move did seem very simplistic, in this light, quick and impossible to deal with though it had seemed before.

"See?" Beth said, proud that she was contributing something. "They totally need to start over. If your reflexes were better, or you ever played video games, you'd have figured this all out already."

Miko briefly looked insulted, but Mina laid a firm hand on her friend's shoulder before she was able to say anything. "Yeah, that's it. We're just not on a Szach level at video games," Mina agreed quickly. "You're really helping out, but ..."

"But you didn't sign the non-disclosure agreement, so we can't let you keep watching this," Miko jumped in. "We'll write down your comments and stuff. Thanks, Munchkin."

"When it comes out, you'll have to tell me. I want to try it, so I can fight ninjas too," Beth insisted, as she was heading back out the door. This time the girls closed it.

There were a few quiet seconds of looking from one to the other, then Miko started watching the video in slow motion, assessing her movements and his responses. "She's right. This isn't a very good martial arts chip ... it's like he's reacting really fast, but doesn't know very many moves."

"Which is why you were kind of doing okay there for a while."

"But you weren't, and I saw you moving, Mina. You're faster than I am. Let me check something."

Mina nodded, and Miko stood up, moving to the center of the room. Miko went through half a dozen sparring moves, and Mina easily countered every one, with Miko seeming to be in slow motion, just like the first fight she'd been in.

"Your chip is way better than his. Or ... way more sophisticated than his," Miko finally concluded.

"But he was still destroying me. I wasn't even close," Mina said.

"Which probably means that what his chip was really designed for was just dealing with someone with your chip," Miko reasoned.

"A simpler chip ... some of the same information ... but not nearly as complex. So ... someone who knew about how my chip worked could program in just a few days, maybe?"

"Yeah, that's what I'm thinking," Miko agreed. "And you remember the classes. Really simple, information-light chips have a lower chance of rejection. There's not as much to conflict with, as long as it's sort of suited."

"That would still take some time, though," Mina reasoned. "Which means that pretty much since the kidnapping, someone has been working on an anti-Inquisition chip. They knew they'd have to deal with us, or figured it out pretty quickly. The programmers probably wouldn't have even thought about it."

"So it's someone who had to deal with the Inquisition before," Miko responded.

"Yeah," Mina agreed. "Or maybe someone who already knew something about it."

"Your boss?" Miko asked.

"Not convinced." Mina replied, with a sigh. "But it's sounding just a tiny bit less crazy now, maybe."

* * * *

The girls had left the Szachs' house, reminding Beth before they left that she was once again sworn to secrecy on threat of never getting to watch anything but little baby stuff again. They had only gotten a few blocks when Mina got a call. "The Director," she explained, on seeing the number. "So, uhm ... stay quiet, I guess?"

Miko nodded, making a zipped lips sign and pulling into a parking lot near a closed grocery to keep car noise out of the conversation. Mina answered the phone. "Yes, Ma'am?"

"Miss Cortez, are you safe?" was the first question, to her surprise.

"Yes, Ma'am. I left the apartment, but I'm safe for now. Trying to figure out where to go next. Should I report in, or ... go to a safe house?" she asked, while tasting aluminum, her chip helping to suggest the safehouse route.

"Absolutely not. Turn off all means of locating you; don't just use our scrambler. I don't want to know where you are, but avoid the safehouses," the Director answered, much to Mina's surprise.

"Ma'am? Avoid the safe houses?"

"You heard me. All of the agents in town have been targeted by someone that knew exactly where they'd be. Agents Park and Hall were found killed three hours ago, after not calling in. I found out about the break in at your apartment while dealing with that. I learned that you'd left the scene, and hoped you'd be able to keep yourself safe until I was able to get to a different location and find a non-Inquisition encryption code to call you from."

While Mina was sure that most of the explanation had some important information in it, she was only half listening from the point she heard about the deaths. "Wait, Ma'am ... Agents ... Park and Hall?"

"Yes, Miss Cortez. Both of them were ambushed after getting a call from a location near them. Someone knew their route, their timing, and the sort of things they'd go in alone on without calling for backup, because it had cues their chips would read as Inquisition business."

"Do we know who?"

"We don't know anything at this point. There was a trace being run at the police station on that license plate you got, but Agent Park was never able to relay the information."

"Wait ... so you ... were running the license plate?" Mina asked, a lot of conflicting information coming between her own brain, her chip, and what the Director was telling her.

"Of course. It was an important lead, improperly gotten or not," the Director assured her, her tone leaving Mina unable to entirely doubt her sincerity.

"I thought ..."

"That you were in trouble? Yes. You were, and eventually, are. And we will deal with that at an appropriate time. I don't send mixed messages. That I didn't ignore what information you got on their operatives does not change the fact that you put yourself in a great deal of danger and disobeyed a direct order. This is not encouraged, and may even have something to do with whoever this is upping the timetable on these attacks. We won't know until we find them."

Mina felt her initial response catch in her throat. Could it really be her fault that the other agents had been killed? She stumbled a few moments trying to find a suitable response before the Director cut off the attempts.

"Whatever you do, do not follow any of your chipped programming regarding going to ground. We have to assume that our entire network is compromised. I'm following some of my own leads and looking into possibly getting some outside help, but I'm having to avoid my typical channels. I also have only limited time to do it, because with my cover identity, I can't disappear for very long. On the other hand, working at the FBI's offices also gives me a certain amount of safety and cover that other agents aren't always afforded.

Gee, thanks, Mina thought. What she actually said was, "That makes sense. When can I expect to hear from you again, and what do I do in the mean time?"

"I'll call once we get an entirely different encryption put in on my end so I can be sure no one is listening. Until then, do not call me; do not come to the office, and keep your head down. If you happen across anything useful, note it, but try to keep your distance."

"I understand, Ma'am," Mina said. With that confirmed, the Director hung up. While Mina would have liked to get in a lot more questions, because relevant information, she felt, might help combat some of her rising panic-mixed-with-grief, she had to assume, from how abrupt the hanging up was, that it came before there was too much risk of someone else gaining something useful from the conversation, if they were listening in or trying to trace it.

"So, that was your boss, huh?" Miko asked.

Mina nodded, tears in her eyes and a lump in her throat still, trying as she was to dispel it.

Miko leaned over to give Mina a hug. "I'm sorry. You were close?"

Mina took a deep breath before nodding. "Agent Park was a really nice guy. He was training me, and my last day with him was stupid and awkward. It was supposed to be better after, and now there's no after. And I didn't know Hall very well ... well, okay, I'd only known either of them since being chipped ... but I saw Agent Park almost every morning. I only saw Agent Hall the once, but ... he was really hot," she finally managed, shoulders shaking a little again with the absurdity of that explanation right now.

Miko hugged her again, then nodded. "Okay, so I know this is a bad time, but sooner or later, someone is going to notice a car in an empty parking lot. We need to go somewhere. There's enough room that we can sleep in the car, I guess ... or we can talk, or whatever you need. Just not here."

Mina nodded, trying to get back in her usual more analytical mind. Without the police records and trace, she had nothing to go on, and much as she was sure it was what the Director wanted, she couldn't bring herself to do absolutely nothing while Scott's kidnappers and her mentor's killers were still out there. She would just need to find a way to do something a little more quietly.

"All right, so we need more information."

"Didn't she just tell you to lay low? Help is coming or something?"

"Yes, but I still don't trust her. Or anyone else who isn't you right now."

"Thanks for the vote of confidence," Miko responded with a smirk.

"Anyway ... yes, she did. I can't just sit on my hands right now though. Especially since I think I can only get this particular bit of information right now."

"Wonderful, so where are we headed?"

"The stupidest possible place in the world ... and just hope that they would never expect me to be quite this dumb."

Chapter Sixteen

Vlad pulled in near the flower shop. Mina wasn't sure if they had any kind of good description of her transportation, but if someone was watching, she wanted to not make it too obvious that she was riding in Vlad. She also hoped to have multiple exits, which the large parking lot in front of the neighboring Mexican restaurant and hardware store had, and Emerald City Flowers and Design didn't.

The girls got out of the car after parking between the two buildings—not a legal parking spot, but out of sight from the street—then scanned the area. Not seeing any signs of anything out of the ordinary, both went to the shop. Mina let herself in with her key and the security code, and went straight to the shop's inventory computer.

"So, I'm dying of curiosity. How are your inventories and receipts going to help us?" Miko asked.

"They're not," Mina responded, logging in as soon as the system finished booting up. "My grandfather was an Inquisitor. I have all of his passwords. Do you have a spare drive I can record all of his information onto? I don't want to stay logged in here any longer than I have to. There shouldn't be anything incoming or outgoing, but still ... if we can just copy everything he had, maybe there's something useful there. We can look at it somewhere else."

Miko agreed, handed over a drive with some of her videos on it, and set to keeping watch on the doors. "I have other copies of those movies," she assured Mina.

"Of course," Mina responded, letting Miko move to take watch while she used the back doors into the hidden system information her chip fed her to pull up her grandfather's records. As soon as they opened, after she'd moved through five different layers of security, she put the chip in and started recording everything.

As she was finishing up, the system chimed, indicating that a new order had come in. "Damn it ... who orders flowers in the middle of the night?" she cursed, finishing the copying and shutting down quickly, to see an e-mail asking for a delivery first thing in the morning ... someone had forgotten her best friend's birthday. Shaking her head at her own curiosity and hitting the shut down, Mina headed for the door. "We need to move."

"You find something?" Miko asked.

"I don't know, but I have the files. Mrs. Cofra forgetting her friend's birthday might have been a big problem though ... if anyone was hacked in enough to look for any activity here."

"Seriously? She ordered flowers in the middle of the night?"

"Yeah, but she also gave me an idea," she responded, opening the refrigeration unit and taking out one of the arrangements slated for delivery early the next day. "My parents will have to figure out something else to take to the Aaronson kid's Chipping Day celebration"

"Okay, so ... flowers, great. I'll ask later," Miko responded.

They got back to the car without any obvious sign they'd been noticed, but no sooner was Miko about to start Vlad up than they noticed a car traveling slowly through the neighborhood, pausing out in front of the shop. A car door opened and shut.

Without waiting for anything further, Miko backed out of the alleyway without turning her headlights on. Typically, when Miko did things like that, Mina wished that Vlad had some of the standard modern safety features installed, so she wouldn't have been able to go anywhere with her lights off after a certain hour. Now, she couldn't be more grateful to be in an antique death trap. They moved slowly out through the back of the lot, through the route typically reserved for delivery trucks from the hardware store, before reaching surface streets. With no sign they'd been followed, they settled on one of the light rail stations with plenty of traffic at all hours.

Mina started going through her grandfather's records, while Miko, in theory, tried to get some sleep. Before that effort really began, she finally asked, "So, I just have to know. Who are we taking flowers to?"

"I'm sorry, Robin," Mina responded. "I need to do one more stupid thing first thing tomorrow morning. *Then* we can try to find a good hiding spot."

"Holy totally not surprised at that scenario, Batman," Miko responded.

"What?"

Miko sighed.

* * * *

Mina spent a while trying to relax, closing her eyes and otherwise trying to clear her mind, but even as tired as she was, sleep simply wouldn't come. She was tempted a few times to call her parents, but elected to keep her phone turned off until the following morning.

She did spend a while checking the information from her grandfather's files. She learned a good deal about the history of the AIA through her grandfather's words, such as confirming that there had been quite a few more agents in those days. There was a lot she didn't understand, either due to coded references an agent of the times may have understood, or simply references to people and events she didn't know. Still, there were some that were fairly clear.

May 25, 2118

Initial evaluation of A. Park is just as expected: he's eager. Very, very eager. This has raised understandable concerns, but I believe them unnecessary. He might need a short leash for his initial missions to prevent trouble, but he'll learn. I gave him the 'chips are a tool, not a crutch' speech, and he seemed to take to it readily. The kid has good instincts, and he trusts them. I respect that. I suspect he'll make a good cop, and I'm confident he'll make a fine agent.

Mina felt tears welling up a bit, more so as her mentor, in note after note, went from the new kid into a seasoned agent. But amidst skimming these, another set of entries caught her eye. The name Fiona Richter (switching in some accounts to Fiona Reisen, then eventually back to

Richter, without much explanation) immediately grabbed her attention. By the notes and her early assessments, she was apparently a fourth-generation Inquisitor. Her father had been killed in the line of duty, after which the AIA had moved her family west from St. Paul. Beyond that, what Mina found surprised her. While Mina read the accounts, a story began to unfold of a technically brilliant new agent who took a case too personally, in her grandfather's written opinion, due to similarities to the case that killed her own father. That case would cost her her arm, and get her put on several months' desk work.

What surprised her the most was one of the later entries.

November 5, 2132

Dear Sirs,

I understand that Agent F. Richter has been offered a promotion, moving her to a supervisory position within the FBI. I was officially asked to submit my opinions on the matter, as her trainer and supervising officer. While she had some rough spots in her early career, particularly the Everett incident, she has been nothing but committed to the Agency. She has so far sacrificed an arm, a kidney, a marriage, and a chance at any kind of normal home life to the AIA. I cannot question her commitment to our goals and ideals.

Additionally, while she has a stated preference for field work, I think her greatest gifts would be realized in a supervisory role. While she has few true friends among the agents, especially those junior to her, she has earned universal respect. Additionally, while her methods may occasionally be graded as unusually harsh, I have no doubt that this is because she genuinely cares for her fellows, and hopes to pass on the lessons she has learned without new agents having to learn them the hard way, as she herself did.

I highly endorse the move, and urge that you do not put too much stock in some other reports, which would cause us to lose a valuable opportunity. We have sufficient agents in the field. An agent managing an agent's responsibilities, while also moving up to a supervisory position with the FBI should be lauded for that accomplishment, and she could do more good for us there.

Sincerely,
T. Escalante

Mina read the note through a couple more times, then went back through a few more accounts. Some of the Director's behavior and attitudes began to make a degree of sense, and as her grandfather had noted, while there was no question that Mina still didn't like Director Richter, she could respect what she'd put into the job. The fact that the Director didn't want to know where she was and had urged her to simply avoid notice helped.

Granted, she was pretty sure that her upcoming plans were anything but careful, but there was something she had to do anyway. She spent a little while writing on the card attached to the flowers, then did her best to cat nap a bit until first light.

* * * *

Because someone involved with the killings of Agents Park and Hall had clearly gotten information on the cops' routes and methods, Mina had Miko keep some distance when she went to the police station where the agents had worked first thing in the morning. She took the flowers with her, delivering them to the station under the guise of bringing flowers to pay respects to the pair of officers who'd been killed. She hoped that even if she was recognized, no one was going to try anything in the actual police station.

She did her best to not tear up or otherwise look like anything but a delivery girl, moving to a cubicle which still bore Agent Park's name. Taking a deep breath, she ducked into it to add her bouquet of flowers to the numerous others decorating the station. No one was looking, and soon Mina was at the keyboard, bypassing the police department's security system like she was, well, perhaps a 'Szach-level' hacker, the taste of aluminum on her tongue.

Rather than looking anything up, however, she entered the license plate from the sandwich shop, and put out a public APB on that plate and vehicles matching the description. She didn't recognize the name of the registered owner when she pulled it up, but was able to enter a falsified report suggesting that it was picked up by a traffic camera leaving the area where the two cops were killed, and the driver was wanted for questioning. She was pretty sure that few things were going to motivate the police like the thought of possible suspects in a cop killing. If nothing else, she was pretty sure that even if that specific car hadn't been there, there was indeed a tie between them, which may lead to other information coming up.

She was tempted to do more than that, but the sound of approaching footsteps drew her attention away. Making sure the report was filed, she turned the computer off, and by the time a policewoman rounded the cubicle doorway, she was back on her feet and rearranging some of the flowers.

"Can I help you, Miss?" the woman asked.

Mina gave her her best smile and shake of her head. "No. Just dropping these off. I'll be on my way. Thank you."

She left the woman behind, but as she neared the door, she picked up the scent of a familiarly cheap cologne. A man was talking into his wrist-comm, though she couldn't pick up what he was saying, but figured that he was either one of the people she'd briefly encountered at the sandwich shop, or shopped at the same place. It was enough to put her on edge. While she was tempted at first to cause a scene to draw attention to him, she knew that would have gotten her kept around for questioning, and she wasn't sure, even here, whom she could trust and whom she couldn't. Instead, she just nodded to him politely as she exited the building. She was still fairly confident, immediately out front of the station, that no one was going to try anything stupid, but she didn't want to lead anyone right back to Miko, either.

Instead, she headed down the block, staying in plain view of people on the sidewalks, moving away from where Miko was parked. She was sure she was being watched, and probably followed, but if so, people were not giving off any of the cues her chip would typically pick up on to suggest where the problems might lie. As such, she continued at a casual pace, as if she hadn't noticed a thing. After crossing one street, she moved with the same casual air to the edge of a building, then quickly darted down the first alley that went through to the next block that she came across.

Somewhere outside the alley, she heard a car suddenly accelerate and turn the corner. It could be coincidence, but she suspected someone was moving to cut off the other end of the alley. She had to either double back or make a run for the next block. Her speed and reflexes would keep her ahead. She knew this ... and she knew it as every breath tasted like chewing on foil. Those aluminum-flavored thoughts hadn't served her well against these particular threats. Mina fought off the instinctive reactions to simply follow the suggestions the chip put in her head and pursued a different plan.

All scents of the city were drowned out by a burning sensation in her sinuses. Nonetheless, she headed for a dumpster at a full run, pulled herself up onto it, sprinted across it, and used the extra height from the dumpster to snag the bottom edge of a fire escape. Pulling herself up, she started scaling the side of the building with the escapes, heading for higher ground. She saw a car pull around to the other end of the alleyway, as she'd expected, while hearing two sets of footsteps entering it from the end she'd come through. She didn't spare much time to glance down, climbing as quickly as she could without making too much noise. After a few moments, she could hear voices below as people shouted to one another from either end of the alleyway. A bit of scuffling as they searched, before a shout told her that someone had seen her.

Mina pulled herself up over the edge of the building just in time to hear a couple of silenced shots pop against the wall just behind her. There was scrambling from below. She suspected it to be people heading into the surrounding buildings to try to cut her off. The combination of burnt-wire smell in her sinuses and the chipped instructions practically screaming for her to get off the rooftops, where someone could trap her, was quickly giving her a headache.

She firmed up her resolve to try to ignore those thoughts, which would lead her right where the counter-chips expected. Despite this, she found herself looking for ways down a few times, simply by merit of the chipped responses being so automatic. Instead, she focused on estimating her best jumping distance and the lengths between buildings, forcing her chip to supply the information. Mina took off at a sprint as soon as she found a span that would be challenging, but not impossible. She cleared the gap across an alley, teetering on the edge of another building, before pitching herself forward.

Picking herself back up, she moved to the best cover she could find and turned her comm on to contact Miko. As she did, it immediately chimed at her to tell her that she had missed three calls from her parents. The sound was followed by another, specifically, someone from an adjoining building yelling "Over there!"

A peek around her cover revealed three people on the rooftop she'd been on, one now sprinting towards her rooftop. Cursing, she stayed as low as she could while heading for another, amidst calls of where she was heading and "Cut her off!"

A couple of shots whined off of the rooftop behind her. She kept running, aware of those following her. Meanwhile, she assumed some of those shouts were into a wrist-comm. Someone—or a bunch of someones—from street level, would be heading to the rooftops in the direction she was moving.

"Miko!" she addressed her wrist-comm, even as she jumped across the gap to another building, now only one rooftop away from running out of block before she reached a street. Her chip helpfully chimed in with a number of routes down, or possible hiding places, which she discarded while also ignoring the urgent insistence that she turn her comm back off.

"Hey. You done doing stupid things now?" came the response.

"Yes. Your turn," Mina called into her wrist as she ran, hearing plenty of movement around her.

"Tracking you now," Miko answered, with the sound of Vlad's engine growling to life in the background.

"Hurry!" Mina added, then quit focusing at all on the comm. She banked to one side, briefly exposing herself to the line of fire. Apparently, that wasn't what had been expected at all, and she managed to leap off the top of her current building towards the row of buildings across the alleyway. This time she didn't quite make it, leaving her dangling by her fingertips from the three story building that backed into the alley. She heard voices below her and glanced down, struggling to pull herself back up. More commotion on the rooftops told her that even if no one would be there to intercept her, someone would have a clear line of fire to her shortly.

She was out of time.

Chapter Seventeen

The roar of Vlad's engine being gunned as Miko tore down the alleyway interrupted the commotion below Mina. While there was enough room between two sets of buildings for delivery trucks, it was never meant to be traversed at that rate of speed. Vlad took a dent to one door, and Miko fought the wheel to keep from spinning as she side swiped a set of garbage·cans.

The next thing she hit was a man with a gun, sending him smashing into the wall. Another dove out of the way of the car. A third would also have gotten clear, but Miko opened the door to catch him as well, though her driver's side window cracked on impact with his skull.

Mina judged the distance, then let go of the rooftop, dropping onto the top of Vlad as it moved under her. "Go, go, go!" she yelled down. She flattened herself to the top of the car, hugging it as best she could. Then she looked up, saw people reaching the edges of rooftops above her, and another figure standing and pointing a gun behind them. Just as the first shots were fired, Vlad cleared the end of the alley and pulled out onto the Seattle streets. Mina almost lost her grip on the car when Miko pulled out of her lane to pass a slower moving car, then barely avoided an oncoming van as she pulled back into the correct lane.

Mina tried shifting herself into position to get to the open passenger side window, but gave up when she heard screeching tires behind them, just as they were starting down a hill. At the bottom of the hill, a large delivery van pulled across the intersection and remained there, with two people quickly climbing out and darting around the van. They were about to be cut off, and even with Miko driving, Mina was pretty sure they couldn't make a turn in time.

"Miko!" she yelled.

"I see it!" came the response and Miko gunned the engine, moving faster, instead of slowing down. Mina's eyes widened, and a glance behind her confirmed that the car behind them had also accelerated to try to keep pace to trap them, making sure they couldn't slow down to turn off anywhere without being clipped.

"Miko!" she yelled again.

"Hold on!"

"Do I have a choice?!"

Mina held on desperately to the top of the car as Vlad sped up, on a collision course with the side of the van, then Miko yanked the wheel about. Countless amounts of time and tire damage trying to perfect the fishtail parking job paid off as the car fishtailed briefly, nearly overturned, then set down on its wheels. Miko grinned like a maniac as she sped back up the hill, and past the car that had been pursuing them. Between the unexpected maneuver, the distraction, and clearly having chips that didn't include stunt driving, the car pursuing them didn't stop in time, slamming at high speed into the van. The maneuver also nearly threw Mina off the roof, but she managed to hang on, though she ended up breaking off one of the side mirrors in the process of trying to find handholds.

Miko turned at the first corner up the hill she could find, stopped there out of apparent line of fire just long enough to let Mina slide in through the passenger side window, then took off again through the mostly quiet streets.

"The cops are going to be after us in no time; you know that, right?" Mina asked, once she found her breath and voice a little.

"Sure, but they'll be swarming that accident scene first. So we have a chance to make our getaway to whatever Batcave you come up with."

"Seriously? Now?"

"There is always time for the Batcave," Miko answered with self-assurance, still glowing from actually finding a practical use for a fishtail turn. Clearly, she'd accomplished a life goal and wasn't going to be dissuaded from being chirpily cheerful, regardless how many people were trying to kill them. Mina did, finally, think to turn her comm back off.

"Fine, okay. We need to get out of the city, away from street cameras, and hope that people were confused enough that no one will get a good look at that little chase until we're clear."

Miko tipped the head of her bobblehead. "I'll make good time, promise."

Mina managed to help navigate, pulling up areas where there were no cameras, back streets slated for repairs, and a route far from the efficient one her chip suggested, but which served her current purposes. Eventually, they managed to make their way out of Seattle and to the more open roads to the south, getting off of major roads and onto the ample stretches of back roads.

"So where are we going?"

"Hobart," Mina answered.

"Where's that?"

"Towards Tiger Mountain."

"What's there?"

"Nothing, that's the point. I just want to get off the road entirely, and up high, then monitor police band for a bit."

"No more stupid stunts leading to car chases and people shooting at us?"

"Nothing planned."

"Damn."

The pair managed to find some backroads remote enough that they weren't even within the road maps included in Mina's chip. They drove back as far as thin dirt roads would allow, into areas that had probably once been occupied, but now were simply part of unofficial hiking and climbing trails. Parking Vlad off the road, Mina got out to stretch and try and relax a little after the harrowing day. Seeing no indication that they'd been followed, she returned to the car, tuning its radio to pick up police band chatter. Unsurprisingly, descriptions of Vlad circulated now and then, and Miko was being sought for questioning.

"That's so cool! I've never been wanted by the police before!" Miko eventually declared.

"Cool 'til your dad hears about it."

"Still cool even then."

"Miko, this is serious. You didn't need to get involved ..."

"Yes, yes, but you're glad I did. You're welcome."

"I'm just worried. I didn't want to get you in trouble."

"We'll manage. We just need to figure out what to do next. Hopefully that whole trip into the police station was worth it."

"That's what I'm listening for, to see if it turns anything up."

"Aha! A method to the madness."

"Well, yes. I don't exactly enjoy being shot at. Or car chases, for that matter."

"Okay, the being shot at was kind of unfair. They need to give you a gun. The car chase was awesome though."

"They'll give me a gun when they think a case merits it," came the automatic response.

"This one doesn't? Wow, I can't wait to see what they consider a case that merits a gun."

"No way. I'm already probably going to be fired. There's no way you're staying involved in this past this case. This is a one-time thing."

"Yeah, like that's going to happen. You had your chance to get rid of me by heading off to Russia and trading your bike for ballet slippers."

"I'm serious."

"So am I."

"Miko, I ..." Mina was cut off by the feeling she should be listening to the police band. A few hours had passed with no word of anything useful, aside from an occasional mention of their exploits. She hadn't even heard anything regarding any of the people in the car or the van that had crashed. Now, there was something about a burned-out wreck of a car being found just off the road in West Seattle. The car was being identified as the one being sought in relation to the dead officers. The car's owner was found with the car, just as burned out. There were no suspects.

"Whoa ..." Miko started. "These guys are hardcore."

"They were trying to kill us not long ago, and killed two cops, remember?"

"Sure, but we're the good guys. We're not their crew. Getting rid of their own evidence trail is something else entirely."

"I ... guess so. But now we're right back to square one."

"Maybe not. We know they're not in West Seattle. That place will be crawling, and they obviously set this up."

"Which also means we need to avoid West Seattle ... so no checking the car out. Not that it's likely to have anything useful."

"Maybe it did. What was the big deal about it before, when you saw it at the sandwich place?"

"It had a university pass, and the people were taken from ... you're a genius!"

"Naturally. Uh, what did I figure out?"

"There'll be a registry for the guy, and his car, at the University."

"The place where there's cameras all over? We're not going to be able to get Vlad anywhere near the place."

"I know, which is why Vlad is going to have to stay hidden as close as we can get, then we're going to steal a car."

"Leave my baby? Wait ... steal a car? The owner won't have the theft tracking turned off. There'll be police all over it as soon as it's reported."

"Sure will. We're not going to be there for long, though, and I'm all for a chance someone else will pick up on some of this in the process of investigating. The entire police department can't be against us, I just don't know who is and isn't on the take is all."

"Clever. So are we going to break into a computer lab, too?"

"No chance. Too easy to just shut down the computers. We're going to ditch the car and go visit your dad."

"You really want me off this case and grounded for life, don't you?"

"I know, I know. You need to make him listen, though. He can get us into the system without raising alarms, and I can find what I need from there."

Miko sighed, weighing the argument. "I'll try. He hasn't been big on listening since ..." Miko trailed off. It had been a fact that loomed.

"Since your Mom. I know, and I'm sorry."

Miko nodded a little. "I lost 1.5 parents. It's hit home every time I try to get him to slow down and pay attention to me."

"If I had anything else ..."

"I know, and you're lucky I'm just that awesome a friend. Let's go. Just give me the directions and where we need to stop." Miko reached out to pat Vlad's dashboard. "I'm sorry, baby. I promise I'll come back for you and fix those nasty dents. We'll go do something special, just the two of us, okay?"

* * * *

They parked a stolen pickup as close to campus as they could without triggering alarms, and covered the rest of the way on foot. Figuring out a route through to Dr. Kimura's office without raising any alarms proved tricky, but Mina hoped that anyone after them would assume she was still laying low in the middle of nowhere somewhere, which was precisely what her brain was telling her to do. She couldn't tell at this point how much was the chip, and the AIA's natural tendencies to try and stay below the radar, and how much was just her brain telling her she really didn't want to die.

They finally reached the back of the Archaeology and Recoveries building, then took advantage of the researchers' preference for fresh air to slip in an open window. Mina spent a few moments waiting to see if there was any sign they'd been noticed, then headed for Dr. Kimura's office. They reached it to find the door open. Inside, Dr. Kimura was alone, packing up his office.

"Dad, what's going on?" Miko asked, before Mina could suggest a more subtle approach.

"Amiko?" he responded, startled. "Where have you been?" he asked, in a tone Mina took as mostly worried. "The police are looking for you."

"Yes, yes. I know, Dad. That's not important right now. We need ..."

"Not important? They've cut off my security clearance, given me a few days off. Whatever is going on, it's serious. We need to go straighten this out." He noticed Mina right behind his daughter as he grabbed his keys. "You've always been the good influence. Want to explain?"

"Dad, we can't go to the police. We can't. That's part of the problem. We need your help."

"Whatever you've done, I'm sure we can explain things to them." He prepared to go, gesturing that they follow. "There's no getting out of this. Let's go, I'll take you myself and put in a good—"

"Dad. Please. Stop. Stop and look at me."

And he did.

"It's not going to work like that," Miko explained. "The police aren't safe. There's someone there that's part of the people who are trying to kill us."

"Why would someone want to kill you?" he asked, not sounding entirely convinced, but at least no longer heading for the door.

"It's tied to Scott's kidnapping." Mina stepped in. "Someone thinks we have more information than we do. She's right, Dr. Kimura. We need your help."

"If this were coming from anyone but you, Mina ..." he started.

"It is coming from me. And do you really think someone would shut off your clearance for traffic violations? Please, we need help," Mina answered, in her best no-nonsense voice.

"You're positive about the police?" He double-checked.

"Someone was high enough to revoke your clearance. We got shot at by people not a block from the police station, and not a word about them has come over police band. Just us. There might be someone I can call, but ..."

Miko looked pleadingly at her father. "There's not a lot of time for questions. Please, please just trust me, Daddy. We don't know where else to go right now."

"Call your contact," he conceded. "We are going to have a very long conversation later, Amiko. Right now ... let's handle right now. My clearance is revoked, but I can log in as one of my colleagues." He hesitated. Mina realized just how serious of an offense that could be if traced.

"I promise, I just need the computer for a few seconds. I need to get some information that will be in the registry to my contact. A lady from the FBI spoke with me, but I haven't been able to reach her again anywhere I'm sure can't be traced."

Dr. Kimura sighed, then went to his desk, plugging in another doctor's name and password, logging into the Archaeology and Recoveries departmental system. Then he stepped away. "Just a few seconds, then you call the lady, and we're going to get you out of here for a little bit. Then I'm going to go ask some questions, once I know you two are safe."

"Dad ..." Miko started.

"I'll be careful. I have a lot of friends and resources of my own. No buts—get what you need. Then we're getting you to a recovery zone."

"Oh ... that's perfect!" Miko responded.

Mina was just sitting down at the computer when she heard the response and looked up, quizzically.

"Recovery zones, like where the viaduct used to be, or the hollows under the stadium. Old Seattle. Dad has the best maps—"

"—including some I haven't logged yet. No one should know you're there," Dr. Kimura agreed. "Or even that 'there' exists."

Mina nodded, smiling just a touch at her first reaction's being not to corner herself like that. A good sign, she figured, that the plan might fly under the radar, at least for a day or two. Right now, she just wanted to buy some time and put the Director on the right path, then get herself to safe ground for a bit.

Turning her attention back to the computer, she traced the car's plates and registry on campus to Raymond Harper. What she was not able to find was any cause whatsoever for him to have a parking pass. Someone rubber-stamped it with no particular notes about his clearance, and his spot was right near the main computer labs. He easily could have passed security checks and gotten to the computer hall without drawing any attention or appearing on camera, as long as someone could bury some of the traffic camera information, or if he had stayed on the campus for more than a day. She couldn't find any notes in the campus registry on how he linked to the University, or what else he did, but she was pretty sure that firm evidence putting him near the kidnapping site would give the Director enough to work with to get some of her other contacts involved. There were too many circumstances now for anyone to dismiss it as something a new hire saw near a sandwich shop.

As soon as she copied the files to Miko's vid chip alongside her grandfather's files, she logged back out and borrowed the phone from the office next door to Dr. Kimura's to call the Director.

"Who's this?" came the response.

"It's me." she said, not giving a name, trusting the Director to recognize her voice.

"Where are you?"

"You told me—"

"I did, and it was the best advice at the time. This is escalating quickly, and the FBI has gotten enough to get involved. I'm going to come take you and your friend into protective custody."

"You know about—"

"You're getting a lot of attention."

"I'm in serious tr—"

"Yes, and we'll discuss that later. Right now, we need to get in front of this and pool our resources. I'm trusting that you wouldn't have come anywhere near Seattle proper if you hadn't thought you had something important to do. Clever putting the car on the police's radar, if dangerous. Unfortunately, leads are disappearing as fast as either of us has been able to put them in front of people. This isn't just a black market operation."

For all that the thought that she still didn't entirely trust the Director and might start her career with another black mark bothered her, Mina couldn't help but feel a little relieved that her leads and information had turned out to be something important after all.

"Where are you?" the Director repeated. "I'll be right there, in person, to come get you."

Mina took a deep breath. She weighed her misgivings against genuinely being desperate for some help and direction. She thought of the endorsements in her grandfather's files. *"Cannot question her commitment,"* he'd said.

"The University. I'll switch my scrambled tracker on for a few seconds in twenty minutes so you can find me when you're close."

"Noted. On my way." The phone hung up. Mina wondered if she'd made the right decision.

Chapter Eighteen

She was pretty sure the call wasn't traced, but in case someone was listening in, Mina, Miko, and Dr. Kimura changed locations, moving to the records building. Dr. Kimura hadn't turned his keys in yet amidst the moving out, so he was able to get into any of the buildings that connected to his work. They kept a close eye out for any eyes on them, but at least as far as Mina could tell, they'd escaped notice for the moment. Dr. Kimura had been quick to agree to go along with anything suggested by a source from the FBI, though he insisted that when help showed up, the girls stay behind him.

After twenty minutes exactly, Mina turned her tracker on, in AIA scrambler mode. While someone could find her by it, they'd have to be checking for it right then after it had been off for quite some time, and she hoped the Director would be close enough by then to get there first. She was relieved when the next voice she heard was, indeed, Director Richter.

"Come on out," she called. "We have four FBI agents and a secure car waiting right outside. We need to go, now."

Mina nodded to the others, and Dr. Kimura walked out first. When there were no gunshots or other signs of problems, and he confirmed the presence of badges and FBI jackets, he waved the girls out of the room they'd hidden down the hall from the main entryway. The Director urged them all forward quickly.

It was only as they were emerging that the trouble started. Mina could at first see only two agents through the doorway. As she came out, she saw the other two, lying on the ground, unconscious. Three others with guns, two men and a woman, were also in the area, but under partial cover. Mina

119

looked at the Director, panicked. As she was about to snap off a comment, she realized that the Director looked as shocked as she did.

"Please come out here and keep your hands visible." one of the FBI agents said, readying his gun, keeping it leveled on the Director. Not seeing any alternatives, the Kimuras started moving towards the group. Mina hesitated, looking for any other option, but saw none that wouldn't place the others in more danger.

"Miss Cortez ..." the Director started, in a warning tone. "Nutcracker, 335," she finished.

Before the words had processed, Mina found herself reflexively diving back through the doorway behind her, sliding across the floor in an arc to find herself behind a stone staircase. She was just coming to her senses, trying to figure out what brought that on, when she heard a pop and a high-pitched whine from beyond the door. She felt dizzy for a moment, but not enough to keep her off her feet. She raced back out, to find the Director kneeling on the ground, her cybernetic arm hanging as a dead weight. Mina's first impression was that she'd been shot in the arm. Everyone else in the area were looking dizzy and off balance, but seemed to be coming around. What's more, suddenly, they were processing in Mina's brain. She was reading stances, assessing recovery time, picking up on where all the guns were. She let her reflexes take her, not fighting off first impressions for the first time in a while.

In a blur of movement, she caught the arm of the FBI agent who had been nearest the door. She wrenched the arm around and over her shoulder so when he reflexively pulled the trigger, he shot one of the other gunmen. Before he could recover, Mina's fist struck a blow under his chin. Catching him as he fell, she used him as a shield to block the gunfire of the first of her opponents to recover their wits. At the second shot, she dropped the agent and tackled the other one low, coming under his gun. A grab and twist to his thumb broke the bone and let her steal his gun. As she was about to point and pull the trigger, the aluminum taste reminded her that FBI agents have their guns coded to them, so she threw it at the next nearest man, instead. His shot went wide as he tried to shield his face. Just enough time for Mina to cover the gap. This time, after a quick disarm, she was able to confirm that the gun wasn't coded to the single user.

Her peripheral vision picked up on Miko, who didn't seem to have been affected by the disorientation the others were suffering, letting her catch the armed woman off guard. As Mina was executing a chop to the gunman's throat, she registered Miko putting her opponent down and taking her gun. Both girls turned to look to where Dr. Kimura was wrestling with the last of the gunman who'd showed up. Two guns were pointed, in case. After all, the Doctor had, to Mina's assessment, suffered the same disorientation as the others, excepting Miko. He may have been disoriented by whatever happened, but he had taught Miko most of her martial arts lessons, and seemed to be handling himself better than the gunman, at least. He dropped his opponent with a combination of a knee to the gut, followed by an uppercut.

"You weren't kidding," he finally said, looking around, moving to recover the gun of the person with whom he'd been wrestling.

Miko darted forward to hug her father as Mina went to check on the Director.

"I'll be fine," the Director answered. "Check the agents and start moving. There will be a ton of security descending on us shortly. Then we need to talk, Miss Cortez."

"Take Amiko with you," Dr. Kimura said, starting to move away from the scene. "I'll lead attention away."

"Daddy, no!" Miko started.

He looked directly at her. "I'll be fine, princess," he told her, with a smile. "I have friends too. We'll talk soon," he promised. "Go with them. Now."

Miko chose not to argue further, moving back towards Mina and Director Richter. The Director spent a few moments looking like she also wanted to argue, but thought better of it on realizing the risk the doctor was taking on their behalf.

"My arm is dead weight until I reboot it," she explained.

Mina confirmed that the two downed FBI agents were alive and breathing, but unconscious.

"Leave them," the Director said flatly. "We need to hurry, and there should be plenty of witnesses soon who aren't on the take."

"What was that, anyway?" Mina asked, as she helped the Director stand and move along with them despite the heavy, immobile arm.

121

"That was a short-range EMP built into my cybernetics. Emergency measures."

"Okay, but what was the rest of that?"

"Duck and cover command. All of our agents have them. I gambled that yours was new enough, they wouldn't pick up on it right away. I had to get some cement between you and the pulse so you'd have a working chip."

"So what else do I have programmed in that you can play Simon Says with?" Mina asked, a bit disturbed by the thought, yet focusing on being grateful for it.

"Very little, I promise. Specifically, nothing that will ever be used outside of emergencies. You have a safe place to go?"

"Yes, but we—"

"Then I'm coming with you. Clearly this goes higher than I thought. We need a plan, and we need to pool our information."

They hijacked a new car, then abandoned it near one of the safehouses, before taking a circuitous route to the excavation zone Dr. Kimura had suggested, where Miko assured them a pair of sporting stadiums used to stand, and elements of them still did in the underground. Miko showed them to her father's supplies, letting them pick up low-light goggles, breathing masks, and gloves. As they went deeper into the underground hollows, Mina started investigating a few of the plaques.

"What is a Big Unit, and why did they have one?"

"It's not a what, it's a who," Miko answered confidently. "It's just a nickname for one of their football players back then."

"Oh."

Miko was able to navigate them reasonably well through the underground remnants of the stadium until they finally found a space that had apparently once been a food court. While the plastic chairs were long since destroyed, some of the rubble suited well enough for the trio to settle in.

"So, what now?" Mina asked the Director. "Is there any other help we can call in?"

"Eventually, yes."

"Eventually?"

"As soon as we get back to my offices, once we figure out a course of action, it will take both of us signing off on an emergency order to get more inquisitorial help. We need additional agents we can trust."

"Doesn't the FBI have security screening procedures and loyalty aptitudes really similar to the AIA's? I was pretty sure that was the cavalry you arrived with originally."

"Yes, and so was I. There is something extremely unusual in this case."

"You don't say?" Mina found herself saying, before she could cut off the sarcasm.

The Director fixed her with a glare. "You should have remained laying low, wherever you were."

"I'm getting that sense, yes. I just needed—"

"You just needed to follow orders. Now we have a civilian in the know, another one involved, and a lot of chaos. This is what happens when agents fly off the handle."

"You mean like you did in Everett?" Mina finally found her voice to challenge a bit.

"Yes, like I did. I was lucky it didn't cost me more than it did."

"You brought me in on this because I have direct knowledge of someone involved in the case! And I've found—"

"We nearly didn't bring you in at all," The Director cut her off.

"So I heard. You recommended against my induction, didn't you?"

"I did," The Director agreed. "Had it not been for Miss Lasko's ringing endorsement and Agent Park's uncertainty overriding my objection, your applications would still be in processing. Agent Park, much as he noted it was a dangerous deviation from protocol, wanted to see Tommy Escalante's granddaughter get her shot, and Miss Lasko thought you were the strongest of our available candidates."

"I'm glad they did."

"If they hadn't, it's possible Agent Park would still be alive."

"A lot of things are possible. We just don't have enough information."

"I agree on that. Unfortunately, this one lead you've been following doggedly from the beginning turned up a dead end. Nicolas Bergen is a small-time thug. Black market ties, yes, but most of his record has been on music discs, bootlegged games, things like that."

"Uhm, who is Nicolas Bergen?"

"The owner of that car. He was the body found dead in it."

"No, the owner of the car is named Raymond Harper."

The Director startled, looking at Mina with renewed interest. "He certainly is not. Where did you find that name?"

"In the University directory. He was the one who put in for the University permit, and got it cleared without entering much of anything into the records. It was like someone just rubber stamped it."

"That's because Raymond Harper is the co-director of University security. He doesn't need to enter anything to clear University campus passes."

"So why didn't we talk to him, instead of Fulton, back during the investigation?"

"We had already spoken with Raymond Harper. He wasn't on duty at the time of the kidnapping. Fulton Hawkins was the security officer on duty. Raymond Harper had to be called in to consult with the Agent on the initial investigation."

"Okay, so Harper still cleared the car with a pass right near the labs. There's no way an electronics smuggler with a record gets passed through like that. Wait ... so, just a thought, but wouldn't bootleg data files and the like be about the perfect place to hide—"

"All sorts of things, yes. Nicolas Bergen also knew plenty of people. He had no record of violence, but some of his known associates certainly did."

"Okay, so someone silenced Nicolas Bergen. My guess would be that unless Raymond Harper's higher up the chain, if someone figures out that I pulled his records, he'd be in trouble."

"And one of our sources of information disappears very quickly, yes. As much as I'd like to tell you to lay low, I think this is going to take both of us. I'll call in backup. As we saw previously, not every agent is corrupt. I'll just need to make sure the call gets plenty of attention."

Miko chimed in, "Mina isn't going anywhere without me. She needs her sidekick."

"Miss Kimura," the Director began, "Your involvement with this case ends right here and now. Whatever your aptitudes and whatever you fancy yourself, you're not an agent."

"I fancy myself someone who has proven to be a help already. What's more, I don't have a chip they already have all the counters for. I take full responsibility."

"As a minor, and a civilian, that's not within your rights."

"My father told me to stick with you guys, and given that they know I'm involved, I might as well make myself useful, right?"

"She has been useful. Some of these guys are programmed to counter everything we do," Mina agreed.

"Very well. There's no time to argue. I'm going to call in backup and provide a distraction. You two need to see if you can locate Raymond Harper and find out what he knows about the death of Agent Hall, and possibly falsified reports."

"Agent Hall? That was the hot one, right?" Miko asked.

Mina shot her a withering glance. "Agent Hall was one of the other agents. He was killed along with Agent Park, the guy who was training me." She glanced to the director. "Where does he tie into this?"

"Agent Hall, under the guise of police work, surveyed the building and gave all security, all exits, and all personnel a pass. He was working with co-security director Harper extensively, so either he was somehow fooled, or ..."

"Or Agent Hall was a traitor." Mina finished.

"Which should be virtually impossible," the Director said.

"Only slightly more impossible than two FBI agents attacking you and two other agents and allying with black marketeers?"

"Something like that," the Director agreed. "As soon as we secure Harper and find out what he knows, we're going back to the offices and filling out an emergency order for additional backup."

"We?"

"Safety measure. As long as there's at least two agents in the field, it takes both to declare a sufficient state of emergency. I would say this qualifies."

"All right, and if Raymond Harper knows something about where the programmers are?"

The Director fixed her with a stare. "Send communications immediately, and follow your instincts. It seems you may be Tommy Escalante's granddaughter after all. So you get a little bit of a leash. Don't push it. Give me a four-minute head start, then find a vehicle and get to the University. We want all possible attention, so feel free to trip some alarms once you get close. I'll keep as much focus off you as possible, as the probable higher-priority target and focal point for more agents arriving."

"Got it." Mina assured her. As the Director headed for the street level, Mina looked to Miko and sighed. "Why do the hot ones always have to be evil?"

* * * *

The girls gave the Director her four minutes, then headed for the street. They quickly found a car Mina could hijack, then Miko took over the driving. She did her best to be inconspicuous until they got near campus, then she found a spot at one edge of the campus. Mina only had to think about the campus layout to get an idea where the main security offices were at.

Mina was about to round a corner to the entrance of the building when she picked up a faint hint of a familiar scent. She froze for a moment.

"Why are we stopping?" Miko asked, glancing about.

"Cheap cologne."

"So we're stopping because we're back in high school?"

"No, no, the Body Spray Wall has a completely different kind of ugh-note. This one's less 'bro' and more 'brute.' The guys at the sandwich shop, and at the apartment wore the same stuff. It's ...not good. Could be someone else, but I don't think we should go in the front door."

"So let's not go in there at all."

"We need to find Raymond Harper, though," Mina reminded her.

"Unless we can find Scott," Miko reminded her. "I have a hunch. The obvious information trail leads to Raymond Harper, but what was it he did as far as his role in all of this?"

"He was working with Agent Hall," Mina reasoned. "Investigating the computer center."

"So if the thugs are split up between trying to find the big, scary lady and dealing with Harper ..."

"Then there can't be many of them there to stop us from taking a look," Mina agreed, changing directions and hugging the building as they backtracked to head for the computer sciences and research center. She made her way in, seeing both the heavily secured path she'd traveled before and other halls leading about the sparsely populated building. Mina remembered the security system and had a feeling that someone had locked out her access. An idea struck her, and she headed for the first door to Scott's old workplace. As she expected, her retinal scan didn't pass. She settled in by the door.

Miko looked at her quizzically. "What are you doing? Can't you just hack through it or override something?"

"I don't need to. I know the local basement troll in residence, and he can get us through everything."

A few moments later, Fulton Hawkins' head peeked out the door. "Agent Cortez? What are you doing here? Everything was cleared before."

"By Co-Director Harper and the police, right?" she asked.

"Well, yes. Is there a problem?"

"Numerous problems, if you haven't noticed the number of security alerts going on upstairs."

"Harper told me not to worry about those."

"Yes, he probably did," Mina agreed. "I need to take a look around this building. This is, uhm, Agent Kimura."

"Yes! A promotion!" Miko answered, quieting when Mina shot her a look.

"She's new," Mina explained. So, you can access everything in the building, right?"

"Well, yes. Most of the work just goes on in my center. We found some temporary backups to maintain the necessities," he explained.

"But there's more building. Did there used to be more computer centers in here as well?"

"A lot more," he agreed. "I'll show you. There's nothing to see. They shut most of it down or moved unnecessary programs into other areas, depending on the discipline they worked most closely with, in order to be better able to keep track of the chipping center."

"I'm sure they did. Just show me the other wings. And quietly. I don't want to set off any more alarms. There's enough going on upstairs."

"What's going on upstairs?" Fulton asked.

"Raymond Harper is being arrested for gross violations of security code and aiding and abetting black marketeers," Mina explained. "Which would be why he told you to ignore the alarms. I'd hate to have to bring you in as an accessory."

"Black marketeering? You're serious?"

"Dead serious," Miko answered. "Now let's get moving."

The halls seemed to go on forever, with numerous abandoned wings, some of them supposedly under construction, with various danger signs. Poking around the first few turned up nothing, but eventually, after what seemed like a mile of twists, turns, and an elevator to another level, Mina paused at one of the construction zones. "Here."

"What's so different about this one?" Fulton asked, clearly confused.

"No dust settled here, and there's an elevator directly up to street level at the end of this hallway, according to the directory."

"Yes, but it's not up to code. They shut it down ages ago when they decided they didn't need a half-broken-down cargo elevator to empty hallways when they moved everything in this wing to the archives building."

"Which would make it perfect," Mina answered, passing the 'Danger' and 'Hard Hat Zone' signs, continuing to follow her nose and the lack of dust until she picked up on signs of greater habitation, and then light peeking out from under a doorway. She gestured, looking sternly at Hawkins.

"There shouldn't be anyone here," he explained lamely.

"Precisely," Mina agreed, looking to Miko. "Ready?"

"As I'm ever going to be," Miko agreed as they approached the door.

Mina readied the gun she'd taken off the thug earlier and moved towards the door. Fulton nervously moved up to the retinal scanner, entering his security codes and pressing his eye to the scan. Fortunately, his clearance apparently was still good for this section, and the door unlocked. As soon as she opened it, Mina was hit with the scent of a lot of people in close quarters, most of whom hadn't had a shower in far too long. A dozen sets of eyes turned towards her as the door opened. Picking up on motion out of the corner of her eye, she ducked back just in time to avoid a shot that cracked off the reinforced plastic frame of the open door.

Mina ducked back around the door, trying to draw a bead on the apparent monitor for the hostages, only to feel herself being dragged back into the hallway by Miko, who frantically pointed towards the back of the room, where another figure was approaching. Mina couldn't doubt he had the counter chipping, as she hadn't even registered his presence in scanning the room, or at least didn't pick out the armed man among the programmers.

She could hear more commotion from inside. "Where would you normally stand to secure a doorway?" Miko asked.

Mina started to point, even as she was fighting the reflex to take her instinctive covering position. "Bait," she saw Miko whispering to her, as her friend ducked just outside the door.

True to Miko's apparent expectations, the big man coming out of the doorway didn't even seem to notice Miko lurking just down the hall, instead immediately turning towards Mina. He kept the door between himself and her, ducking around it to take a shot. Before he could pull the trigger, Miko kicked the back of his knee, causing it to buckle and making the shot go wild.

Miko tried to follow it up while he was off balance, but even with surprise, he was too fast for her, recovering his balance and whirling about. Before he could pistol whip Miko, Mina managed to dart forward and grab his gun arm. She kept a death grip on his arm even as he came back about, swinging his off hand right past Mina's guard. She felt the fist on her nose, and the taste of blood, her vision blurring, but still she held on so he couldn't get his gun free.

While he was occupied with Mina, Miko got a second chance, sweeping his legs and using that momentum to drive the man's head into the wall. He staggered back after the impact, trying to clear his vision. This time, Mina was able to get a clear shot without risk of hitting Miko, and managed to shoot him in the chest while he was finding his equilibrium.

"Look out!" Miko shouted, as the second figure emerged into the hall. It was all she was able to say before a pistol butt caught her between the eyes.

"Miko!" Mina shouted, charging at the figure. She managed to close the gap before he could get a shot off, driving the man back into the room before he caught his balance, though that was all she managed, as he managed to backpedal and shift to one side before she could bring him down.

With Beth's warnings about video games passing through her head, as Mina's reflexes screamed *'left!'* and she started to shift that way, she managed to jerk right instead. It was less the graceful dodge it should have been than an ugly tumble due to the effort to fight her own instinctive maneuvers, but to her surprise, it worked. The man lunged right past her, striking thin air where her head should have been. Unfortunately, the tumble didn't leave her in a good position to counterattack, but it bought her time. Mina swept at his legs, kicking him in the shin and causing his knee to hyperextend, sending him tumbling back into one of the work stations. She was trying to scramble to her feet when she saw him adjusting, leveling his gun. Just before he could fire, there was a tremendous crash, the sound of electricity and breaking glass, then screams accompanied by burning smells.

Head still swimming a little, Mina caught sight of Scott standing just behind where the guard had been, his eye still jacked into the computer, now missing the monitor that Scott had clubbed the guard with. "Mina?" he asked. "What are you doing here?"

Chapter Nineteen

The programmers had all been tethered to their stations. Apparently, there were normally four guards on duty, but two had recently left. When it was clear that Miko was all right, Mina, Miko and Fulton started working on freeing everyone. A double check of the cargo elevator revealed it to be in perfect working order, despite signs stating that it should be otherwise.

"How many of those chips did they have you make?" Mina asked Scott as they were moving.

"Not very many. We managed to sabotage the first batch before they caught on somehow."

"Any idea how?"

"Testing, probably. They weren't very good—real rush jobs."

"Just like video games. No complete programs, just a speed setting and specific set of counters?" Mina filled in.

"Exactly," he agreed. "And anyone using them would be at high risk for eventual rejection."

"Wonder how many of them know that?' Mina mused. "Can you help us confirm all copies are accounted for?"

"Yeah, we couldn't get any outside data chips or anything, but I've been storing a backup copy in my eye. Get me to any computer with enough juice to run this, and enough security it won't get out, and I'll be able to come up with a list for you."

"You said something about testing? We've been having trouble with a couple of rogue FBI agents and ..."

"And police officers?" Scott asked.

"How did you know?"

"Because that's how they moved us all. A cop showed up, said something to our boss about compromised security settings, and insisted we all had to come with him and evacuate to a secure lab. The boss confirmed it, told us all to go along. We never saw him again, but I'm pretty sure he was in on it anyway."

"Why would you say that?"

"Because that's what we were arguing about. He was messing with some data transfers I was pretty sure he shouldn't have been. Trouble was, he knew I knew. He reported me for trying to hack the system, and blamed me for the things he'd been doing."

"How did you figure it out?"

Scott blushed. "I actually was hacking the system a little. Only because Hawkins kept having trouble with my security codes. I got locked out of the system a few times, and he kept having to readjust things for the new guy. I was trying to figure out why it was doing that, and ran into someone else messing with it. I tracked a bunch of quick changes to the security offices, but was kind of stuck, since to report anything to Hawkins and Harper, I would have had to say how I knew. I didn't begin to suspect it was anything like this."

"Even if he was in on it, I don't think your boss knew what he was getting into either," Mina reported. "He's dead."

Scott paused. "Dead?"

"He's not the only one. Those rush jobs have been wreaking havoc. If we're thinking of the right person, the cop who evacuated you all is dead too—so is his partner. Can you tell me what he looked like?"

"Was he hot?" Miko chimed in, from where she followed close by, looking in good spirits despite her quickly developing black eye.

Mina was blushing too hard to look daggers at her again. "Will you knock it off with that?" she finally said.

"Hey, he was your evil boyfriend. Evil boyfriends are totally not my type."

"How would you know? You never saw him."

"I just know these things, okay? I'm pretty sure he didn't look like John Belushi, and if he didn't have the eyes of doom, he was totally not my type. Besides, evil," Miko answered quickly, deflecting the comment like pretty much every other time boys came up.

Mina just shook her head. "Hopeless."

"Am not. I'm the chirpy optimist sidekick. You're the grim floral avenger," Miko answered back, losing none of her good cheer.

Finally, Mina couldn't help but laugh. "Floral Avenger, seriously?"

They were interrupted by Hawkins, racing after them as they were about to emerge out onto the main campus. "Uhm, agent folks ... there's a serious problem. I wouldn't go out there. Some kind of shootout, and nothing is getting off campus. I was trying to confirm what Agent Cortez was saying. I think Raymond Harper, or someone, has everything all jammed up. There's some kind of signals going around, all closed network. I'm pretty sure there's people headed this way."

"Then we need to get a signal out, and we need to keep these people safe," Mina declared, looking between the programmers. "How quickly could you guys change the security settings for the security system? If you sealed yourself in, and changed the authorizations ..."

"They'd need a tank to get in after us," Scott said. He and Hawkins got the rest of the group turned around, heading back for their old workstations.

"You coming, Mina?" he asked, noticing her starting back in the original direction.

"I can't," Mina said. "You guys have to get people here—the cops, the FBI, anyone, everyone. Lots of attention—not just a couple of officers either. I need to go find my boss. I almost didn't call her in at all, and now she's pinned down out there somewhere buying us time. I need to go help her."

"Then I'm coming with you," Miko declared.

"Not this time. You're still wobbly, probably have a concussion. Go and keep Scott and the others safe, just in case."

"You need me," Miko insisted, though she sounded a little less sure of herself than usual. Apparently, the comment on still being wobbly on her feet hit home.

"I need you safe, and I need the data in Scott's eye. You need to keep an eye on them and make sure they get locked in safely."

"You sure you're going to be all right?"

"No," Mina admitted. "But there's just some things the Floral

Avenger has got to do."

* * * *

If what Scott had said was true, Mina was pretty sure there couldn't be that many people out there with the anti-Inquisitor chips. On the other hand, on checking her gun, she only had seven shots left. On emerging from the building, she could hear an exchange of gunfire from some distance away. She couldn't initially get a good fix on it, with the echoes off the old stone buildings, but did her best to navigate towards it while hugging buildings and peeking around corners. As much as she was in a hurry, she couldn't do the Director any good if she got herself shot.

Along the way, she tried to raise her own commotion, and to maybe draw some attention off of the Director, smashing in windows of buildings and cars alike. Car alarms going off diminished some of the ability to hear the occasional gunfire, but she was sure they'd also get attention in their own right. She didn't linger long, and whenever she identified camera emplacements, she did her best to avoid them, though she was forced to spend two shots taking out a pair of the wide-angle security cameras, lest someone pinpoint her exact location. She wanted to try and draw some attention away from the Director, but was only willing to take so many risks. If she got herself caught, she wouldn't do anyone any good.

A few times she considered trying to head into one of the taller buildings to see if she could get a crow's eye view of the goings-on elsewhere, but this time she listened to the chip's instructions, and chose not to risk getting herself cornered atop a building, if she got caught on any of the indoor cameras. With only five shots left, she wasn't going to hold anyone off for very long.

Finally, she came out on a hill where she could see some hint of the source of the noises. There were two cars crashed together, forming a V. From the hilltop, she could see a figure crouched down in the crook of the V. The Director, likely. She was surrounded by at least four people Mina could see at different points down below. All had taken cover around the buildings that bordered the parking area.

She didn't see any easy way to get to the Director, or approach the people's covered points without drawing attention to herself, and while she saw four, there could easily be more she couldn't see. If she had had a rifle, she might be able to provide a bit of covering fire, or catch one person by surprise, but the pistol wasn't going to cut it. While she was confident that Scott and the rest would figure out a way to get past whatever was cutting them off and get help, she had to figure out a way to buy some time. She also knew she didn't have a lot of time to figure it out. While several ideas occurred to her, accompanied by the now-familiar aluminum taste, she discarded those, since anything that was going to come via her chip would have been accounted for. She had to think as something other than an Inquisitor.

Her face broke out into a grin as a thought occurred. If she couldn't think like an Inquisitor, she did know how to think like a landscaper. The parking areas bordering campus had been part of the beautification processes. The University had fields and flower beds and lawns, all of which needed maintaining. All of that took supplies.

She bolted out across open grass, headed for the area where they kept the maintenance truck. She'd driven one like it a few times—slow and ponderous, more good for hauling irrigation equipment, sod, or whole trees than it was for any kind of maneuvering. It would serve her purposes perfectly.

Mina broke into the shed and uncurled all of the gardening hose in the place, tying it everywhere she could find a secure place about the supply shed. The other ends of the hose she ran out to the truck, tying it about the towing hitch and anywhere else she could find to tie it off. Then all of the towing chain and every bit of rope she could find was used as well. Before closing the shed, she grabbed a pair of respirator masks, and two sets of goggles, pulling one set on.

She hotwired the truck and started to pull. At first the wheels just dug in, dirt shooting back in a rooster tail behind her, but at last they found purchase, and the shed broke off its foundations, towed behind the heavy truck.

Just as she was celebrating her victory over the foundations, she saw two cars coming at her. Both jumped the curb, coming fast across the lawns. Mina gunned the engine, heading straight towards them. The thick windshield cracked as bullets came at her from the oncoming cars, then splintered in at the next shot, making her shield her eyes for a moment and duck as low as she could. She jerked the wheel hard to the side, at first getting only a sluggish response, but eventually, she turned, barreling right at one of the cars. It lost its traction in the grass, skidding out of the way as she passed the other, her passenger side window blowing in with a shot. She could see in her side view both cars recovering and turning to pursue. They'd catch up with her soon enough—she was just trying to get to the top of the hill before they did.

She swerved side to side, causing the shed to almost tip a few times, making it hard to get around the small building. One car finally did, racing up to pull alongside her. She jerked her steering wheel again, her heavy truck crashing into the car's side, and a bullet ricocheted off the frame of her driver's side window. The car fell behind again as its driver recovered from the side swipe.

A few more shots rang off her frame, throwing up sparks and sending more glass flying. Mina could feel something warm on her face, her chip helping make her aware she was bleeding from one of the sprays of glass. Shoving thoughts of injuries aside, she pushed on, reaching the hill. Once she got over the top, gravity took over. Mina did her best to steer at first, until she got good momentum going on the hill. When gas was no longer needed, she turned the truck at a diagonal, heading for one of the buildings, then opened the driver's side door. She pulled herself up out of the cab, and managed to climb around into the pickup bed. Balancing as best she could, she darted across and dove off the truck in a roll just as it careened into the side of the building. Mina rolled with the impact, ending up tumbling down the hill. She heard shouts of alarm, looking back to see the truck skidding along the front of the building towards one of the gunmen's secure points. Eventually, the front of the truck snagged, spinning it around. The shed being towed came with it, crashing into the side of the building. Mina went racing for the cover of the nearest vehicles as the shed hit the wall near one of the gunmen, and the wooden building exploded in a rain of gardening tools, splinters, fertilizer, bark, pesticides and who knew what else. The truck continued to spin out, chains and hose whipping out behind it. Briefly, Mina hoped it might literally explode, like in some of the movies, but even without anything going up in flames, it was a pretty spectacular collision.

Amidst the chaos, she caught sight of a male figure emerging from one of the covered points some way away, trying to figure out what was going on. Aiming as best she could through the thick haze of dust and fertilizer in the air, Mina fired, dropping him and clearing her path.

Someone would figure out what was happening before too long, but for the moment, she had cover and confusion, and anyone not wearing a mask probably wouldn't be doing so well. Mina emerged from her cover and darted towards the Director's hiding spot in the V of the two crashed cars. She had almost made it, when the sound of screeching tires caught her attention. She managed to dart out of the road enough to not get run over, but felt an intense pain in her leg as a bullet tore into it and Mina tumbled to the ground, landed on her back and clutched her injured leg. The pursuing cars rushed past her down the hill. My God, she'd been shot! The wound didn't hurt as much as she thought it should, and somewhere in the haze starting to overwhelm her brain, the chipped thoughts told her she was going into shock. She let the chip help push her into auto-pilot, crawling and fighting to get to her feet and get to cover, while she tried to clear her head.

The vehicle was starting to turn about, her pursuers ready to take another shot when Mina saw the Director stand and fire a shotgun from the hip. The car spun out, and the front windshield appeared to be painted in red.

Mina pulled herself up onto one leg, and hop-scrambled as best she could, diving onto the hood of one of the cars in the V, where the Director caught her hand and pulled her across.

"You really don't know the meaning of subtle, do you, Agent Cortez?" the woman asked. From her tone, it took Mina a moment to realize that Fiona Richter had just made a joke.

"No, Ma'am. But I know how to make an entrance," she said, pushing the spare respirator and goggles towards the Director.

"Did you secure Raymond Harper, by chance?" the Direcor, asked while pulling on the gear. "I haven't been able to get through to anyone."

"I did one better. The programmers are rescued and under heavy security. I came to find you. They're working on getting past the jamming to get help here. With all of them working on it, it shouldn't be much longer."

Your stunt bought some time, but I don't think this is going to hold out much longer. How many shots do you have left?"

"Four. How many of them are out there?"

"At least seven. Or there were. Plus however many in the cars pursuing you. Did you learn anything else from your rescue, by chance?"

"If we can get Scott to a secure computer, he has an account of how many of these chips got out. He doesn't think there's very many. We're probably seeing most of it."

"This may be enough."

"Maybe, but we've thinned their numbers some, and numbers help."

"Yes, they do. And they have them."

"No, no ... not like that. This is ... like a video game."

"Explain."

"Their chips counter everything ours are feeding us, but they're not very sophisticated. They kind of fix on one action at a time," Mina explained, while doing her best to tear the sleeve off of her jacket to wrap around her leg, simultaneously grateful she was starting to process better, less so that the gunshot was starting to hurt a lot more. "If you can do something they actually don't expect and divide their attention, well, it sort of glitches."

"And we don't need to stop them all, we just need to buy a little more time for your friends."

"Precisely. I'm a little low on ideas, though."

"Did anything in your apparently extensive reading tell you how I lost my arm, Agent Cortez?"

"No, Ma'am."

"Please follow me as quickly as you can. It went a little something like this." Fiona Richter stood from her hiding spot, firing at the first sign of motion, then rushed into the cloud. Mina did her best to keep up, noticing the Director hunching low and leading with her cybernetic arm. She could hear more gunfire, and once felt something graze her shoulder, but nothing solid. They reached one of the hard points, finding two men trying to draw a line of fire through the thick haze. The Director fired her shotgun, but by the time she brought it about on them, they'd adjusted to her line of fire. Mina got the idea, whirling about and putting two bullets into one of the men before he adjusted to her as well.

She was turning on the other, but he had her beat to the draw. She fired, but nowhere near on target. He would have had her dead to rights, had the Director not whirled about, using the shotgun as a club, connecting with the man's neck. There was a strangled sound, then another as the surprised gasp caused him to inhale a lungful of fertilizer. Mina shot him point blank, and only then noticed the Director's arm hanging limply, with newly exposed and sparking circuitry in a number of spots. Mina traded her the shotgun for the pistol and used the last shell in the shotgun to blow the lock off the nearest door. They charged into the building, emerging from the haze.

"Up the stairs," Mina suggested. "And hope no one is on the cameras."

"If we head up, there'll be no way down."

"Which they also know," Mina reminded her. "It took them a while to look up last time."

"Reasonable, under the circumstances," The Director agreed, as the pair headed for the fire stairs.

With Mina's injured leg and the Director's deadweight arm, getting up even a flight proved to be a major chore. Mina was starting to feel faint by the time they'd gotten up four flights. The Director grabbed hold of her with her good arm, pulling Mina along up the last flight until they emerged onto the roof. They took what cover was available, with the Director keeping aim on the one doorway to the rooftop. Mina tried to pull herself into position to aim the shotgun, but the dizziness grew worse.

She wasn't sure at first if it was just ringing in her ears, or the lights flashing in front of her eyes, but the noise eventually grew into sirens. Mina vaguely heard the sound of the Director's comm crackling to life.

"Miss Richter, please advise."

"Supervisory Agent Richter to all units, surround the area, full net. Don't let anyone escape. Most especially Raymond Harper."

Chapter Twenty

Mina woke up in bed. She felt weak, and it took a while for the haze to clear from her thoughts. At first, she thought she might be in the hospital, given the type of bed, and the fact she had an IV drip. As she became a bit more aware of her surroundings, she noticed Miko and Scott sitting next to the bed, talking quietly. "Where?" she started, quietly, trying to sit up with mixed success.

"Hey, Sleepyhead," Miko chirped, turning her attention to Mina. "We were wondering how long it was going to take you to get up on one of those rare times you get to sleep in." She checked her chrono, then glanced at Scott. "I win. You owe me five bucks."

"You couldn't have woken up five minutes earlier?" Scott mock grumbled, though he couldn't hide the smile. "We were worried about you."

"So, where am I? Mina repeated. "Are my parents around? They have to be worried sick,"

"FBI HQ basement. Your parents have been told you're in protective custody until an investigation finishes, then you're being released," Scott informed her.

Miko added, "Oh, yeah—released with strict orders for no heavy biking or anything for a couple weeks. They've got you patched up pretty good, dermal patching, blood transfusion, the works, but you can't aggravate it. They'll just have to let you use the truck." Miko grinned a bit wider. "Though based on the state of campus, I'm not sure you should be allowed to drive. Like, ever."

"Ok, so when exactly am I being released?"

"We're all stuck here for a while. Your Director and Miss Lasko wanted to be informed when you woke up. They need to figure out what they're doing now with the information Scott saved."

"Exactly what did you find?" Mina asked, managing to sit up, forgetting all about her leg feeling numbed or the fuzziness in her head.

"It's not good," Scott admitted. "Almost all of them are accounted for. They're pretty sure Harper was high up, but suspect some black marketeer is still out there calling the shots. Still no idea how they got to cops, FBI agents and one of your people. Worst thing, though, is that two chips are still missing. While there's not a lot of facilities that can make high grade chips, if they have even one to copy, you could end up eventually seeing a lot more of those things."

Mina nodded. "The Director mentioned an emergency order. Bringing more people in on this."

"You're probably going to have to," Scott agreed. "Starting with just going through everything at the University and Harper's records to try and figure out where things fell apart."

"His records?"

"Raymond Harper shot himself, rather than letting himself be taken in," Scott informed her. "They're going to have me working on hacking his files more soon, but so far, it doesn't look promising."

"You've been busy."

"You've been out for almost 24 hours."

"Then its time I get back to work," Mina responded, struggling to turn.

Miko grabbed her shoulder and stopped her. "Uhm, hospital gown," Miko said quietly. "Let Scott go let them know you're up so they can come remove the IV and do this right ... the Floral Avenger should not be fighting crime without pants."

* * * *

The Director was waiting for the three of them when Mina, Miko and Scott showed up in her office. Her movements suggested to Mina that she'd also spent some time being patched up, and her artificial arm was still in bad shape, but Mina was still pretty sure the Director was taking better to her recovery than Mina. She did her best, despite the limp and all that had happened the last few days to look as professional as possible, standing in front of Fiona Richter's massive desk. "Agent Cortez, reporting for duty, Ma'am."

The Director fixed her with a stern gaze for a few moments, then sighed, relaxing just a little. "We have quite the mess here, Miss Cortez."

"I know, and I know I didn't always help matters. I'm sorry, Ma'am." Mina started, wondering again if she was going to keep her job, or if she might end up transferred somewhere, like the Director had been before her.

"I appreciate you taking responsibility for your actions, Miss Cortez. Learning on the job can be a tricky experience. We'd have preferred you to have a lot more training before putting you on an investigation. You could use more patience, and there's going to be a lot of questions from high up on Miss Kimura's presence in this investigation."

Mina nodded. "I understand, Ma'am."

"That said," the Director continued, "You showed some good instincts. In your own unique fashion, you did also save my life on campus. Trying to clean and cover that up is going to take half the department, but I'm grateful. Unfortunately, the case isn't solved, and we seem to have hit a dead end."

Mina relaxed just a little at the hints of praise. "That's what I was told. Two chips still missing, and a dead end as to who Raymond Harper was answering to, right?"

"Precisely. Meanwhile, neither you nor I are in condition to pursue this to the best of our abilities. Besides, with all the attention they've drawn, the black marketeers involved are most likely to try and get very far away from here. They won't want to give us anything to follow up on, so the danger should be past."

"So you're pretty sure it is black marketeers, Ma'am?"

"We've identified most of the people captured or killed at the University, as well the burglar at your apartment. While there are some exceptions, almost all of them have extensive ties with smuggling rings or other major criminal enterprises."

"Exceptions, Ma'am?"

"We kept everyone who responded on site, and started a live sweep for the missing chips, since we had the testing center right there at the

University. In addition to the two rogue FBI agents from before, one additional agent and two police officers were found to possess the counter-chips. We thankfully managed to have enough attention on it that they weren't able to get away, nor interfere overmuch with the investigation, though we caught the agent in particular trying to be sure she was the one taking possession of Harper's records. Both the local FBI offices and all local police precincts are undergoing an extensive sweep in our search for the remaining chips, or someone who can shed some light on the mole's location."

Mina took all of this in, but found she had nothing to add this time. "So you're going to put out the emergency request, and have me sign off on it?"

"Right after we talk to Miss Lasko," the Director agreed. "She's preparing the paperwork, at my request, and assures me she'll deal with the political fallout. We need to replace our own population, and make sure we have every possible resource to address the threat."

"Understood, and I totally agree. I mean, not that it necessarily matters that much, but this is way beyond me," Mina admitted.

"Don't be too hard on yourself, Miss Cortez," the Director answered. "That's my job," she added, with a completely straight expression. "Besides, this has gone well beyond what any of us could have expected."

"So, before we go speak to Miss Lasko, what happens with Scott and Miko now?" Mina asked.

The Director looked over the other two, so far standing quietly just a bit behind Mina. "Mr. Szach isn't a problem. His security clearance is more than sufficient. He'll have a few questions to answer regarding some University records, but I don't think that will ultimately be a problem. For now, we're retaining his services as a consultant."

"Well ... that's something. What about Miko?"

"Miss Kimura is a different matter entirely. Thankfully, while it always gets plenty of unpleasant questions, the situation isn't without precedent. There is also the matter that her father works with University and historical records, which includes some sensitive information at times. That's not saying there won't be a lot of scrutiny for a while, but I think it can be dealt with. In any case, she's still part of the process for now, as Miss Lasko wanted to debrief her as well."

"Kinky." Mina heard Miko mumbling under her breath.

* * * *

Miss Lasko was settled behind her desk when the four entered. Though she offered them a seat, the Director declined, apparently feeling it more official to deliver reports standing, as she'd had Mina doing when Director Richter was the one on the other side of the desk. Despite the hints of pain and remaining numbness in her leg, Mina followed suit. As soon as she entered the room, Mina paused, trying to figure out what was different about Miss Lasko, and quickly ascribed the unease to the total change of atmosphere. Where before, the office had been welcoming and the woman friendly, now, Miss Lasko was all business. "What do we know?"

"We've accounted for all but two of the chips and locked down the University's computers. Raymond Harper seemed to have been heading things up at the University, but someone was feeding him his marching orders," the Director explained.

"I received reports of corrupt FBI agents?" Miss Lasko asked.

"Unfortunately, correct," The Director confirmed. "Three FBI agents, two police officers, and one inquisitor."

Mina fidgeted at the last bit, shifting a little uneasily on her leg. She glanced back to Miko and Scott, both of whom seemed to be trying to be quiet and out of the way, difficult as that was.

"An AIA Agent? That's a serious problem," Miss Lasko continued. "You're positive? That should be virtually impossible."

"Virtually," The Director said. "We have Agent Victor Hall linked to Raymond Harper, and his reports stated that the University computer and programming center had been checked end to end, and was clear. That was obviously not the case."

"You have no idea what an agent would stand to gain from such associations?"

"None. His accounts were under observation, like all agents. His psychological profile was solid. His profile and record to that point showed an absolute dedication to the ideals the AIA was founded under. He'd even had family in the service," the Director explained.

A lot like herself. Mina couldn't help thinking, and the thought made her that much more uncomfortable. She didn't care for every detail of her current job, perhaps, but she couldn't imagine betraying national—international—security. The line of thought continued to add to her unease. The conversation continued as she tried to place what was bothering her.

Her attention was briefly dragged back by the commentary. "Agent Cortez has agreed to sign off on the emergency order," the Director was explaining. "I hesitate to do it, given the amount of attention and expense, but until those chips are located, we have a massive threat to every asset in the agency. "

"If you're certain it's necessary, I'll do my part," Miss Lasko agreed. "You don't serve as a Deputy Mayor for this long without knowing how to muster the bureaucracy so people can do their job. What kind of numbers are we talking?"

"It's a matter of international security at this point," The Director answered. "As many as it takes to follow every lead, crack down on every black market outlet we have traces on, interrogation specialists to talk to the captured FBI agents and police officers. We simply cannot afford to give them any time to figure out duplication of the chips, or we're going to start losing more agents."

Mina focused on that a moment, something in the words sticking out. The word security, in particular hit her oddly, then was accompanied by the smell of expensive cologne and gun oil.

Mina started to twitch, then forced herself to be still, glancing at Miko instead, as she'd done moments before. In this glance, she took note of Miss Lasko's two bodyguards, the broad-shouldered giant, and the smaller Japanese man she'd seen on her first visit to this office.

For a moment, it made perfect sense they'd be there. It was a dangerous situation, after all. Someone with Miss Lasko's history and ties to the AIA would be very vulnerable. Then it began to hit her. She knew the men were armed. They still smelled the same. Previously, even Miko had noted that the big man stood out as someone who could handle himself. Despite which, she'd overlooked their presence.

Mina lightly nudged Miko, not saying a word, nor gesturing, just making sure her friend was alert.

Miss Lasko glanced at Mina curiously. Mina had been distracted enough to lose track of if she was still being discussed, or if she'd missed something. "I'm sorry," she started.

"Quite all right. Injured in the line of duty, I understand. I will be looking forward to reading the reports in more detail. It seems maybe we made a good decision bringing you in after all," Miss Lasko said, smiling warmly at Mina. "I'm sorry your introduction to the job has been so rough."

"I understand I have you to thank for getting me in on this case," Mina answered.

"I'm not certain whether to say you're welcome or I'm sorry, but I am glad we got your friend and the rest of the programmers back safe and sound."

"Oh, no question. So am I," Mina said. "You know, it's just one of those things. I've been shot, had people chasing me, wasn't sure who to trust. It's just been kind of a rough few days. I don't mean to sound ungrateful," Mina meandered, looking to the Director as she continued. "I do appreciate what you guys have done for me. On the other hand, I could have been in Russia dancing the Nutcracker right now."

The room burst into motion.

Chapter Twenty-One

Mina's shifts and twitchiness, it seems, had already registered to the security detail. Both went for their guns, but the Director picked up on the hint faster, and activated the EMP pulse in her cyber-arm. There was an electrical crackle and a pop. The next instant, Mina nearly lost her balance as the whole world seemed to shift into confusing rapid motion. She had trouble tracking movement; she was nauseous, and a crushing headache spread from the base of her neck up the back of her head. She was glad the Director had caught the "Nutcracker" hint, and even more glad that everyone else in the room, aside from Miko, was having just as much trouble as Mina.

The bigger man stumbled forward, drawing a gun despite the pulse, probably having some actual combat training entirely outside of his chip. Still, his motions were uncoordinated. Miko caught his gun hand, disarming him even as she translated the momentum from his stumbling rush into an aikido throw, slamming his head into Miss Lasko's desk, cracking the thick wooden surface.

The smaller man on the security detail was too far away for Miko to reach easily. He had his gun out, pointing it in Mina's direction, since she was the one who'd originally drawn their notice. The Director managed to crash into him despite her dead weight cybernetics, throwing his aim off enough that the bullet whistled past Mina's face. With both working without chips, and the Director hindered by the weight of her limb, the man was able to crack his pistol across her face, dropping her to the floor. Mina was able to cross the space in that time, grabbing for his gun arm. She caught it, managing to force another shot wide. Scott joined her in grappling with the man, finally catching up enough with what was going on to react. Even with both of them together, he managed to struggle free, knocking Scott down and shoving Mina back towards the front door.

The struggles had bought Miko enough time to get close. He swung at her, Miko ducked under the punch, then came up with a punch to his throat. He gagged and staggered. When his hand came up to try and defend himself from another strike, she grabbed his hand, putting him in a wristlock before sweeping his feet. "I've got this one, don't let her escape!" Miko called, still continuing to track the movement of the world better than anyone else in the room.

Mina glanced up, seeing Miss Lasko coming at her, trying to get to the door. Mina almost failed to react in time, still feeling like she was moving through molasses compared to the perceptions she'd grown used to. She managed to grab Miss Lasko's hair, dragging her back through the doorway and setting her staggering back. Miss Lasko swung wild, telegraphing her punch enough that even in her current state, Mina was able to duck her head back. She cocked her fist back and swung as hard as she could. Mina's fist connected, and Lasko dropped to the floor, not moving.

Mina barely noticed, clutching at her hand. "Ow! Damnit."

"Wow, that might have been the worst punch I've ever seen," Miko said, looking up from where she was keeping the bodyguard trapped in the wristlock. "Dude, quit struggling, you're going to—" there was a pop. "—Break your wrist. Now hold still." The struggling stopped.

The Director was slowly pulling herself to her feet. "Miss Cortez, I do hope you have an excellent explanation for what just happened, or we will have a lot of explaining to do."

"No," Mina answered, gesturing to the bodyguard Miko had in the wristlock, then the man unconscious, draped over Lasko's broken desk. "We have our final two chips, which means Miss Lasko has a lot of explaining to do."

* * * *

Miss Lasko came to not long after. By that point, Director Richter had managed to get more FBI agents on the scene. Their confusion made

Mina very glad that the Director was the first one speaking to them. Had Miss Lasko gotten to the same agents first, everything might have gone very differently. The two bodyguards were taken down to be tested to verify the presence of the missing chips, though Mina had no doubt. As she saw Lasko stirring, she had just one question. "Why?" The how, when, who and the rest would come out in time. Mina just had to know what had been worth all the lives.

Miss Lasko looked around, as if considering a few moments. She glanced to her computer, which Scott was already heading towards, with no one making any effort to stop him. With a sigh, amidst efforts to drag herself back to her feet, Lasko replied.

"I'm sure you think I'm a terrible, callous person. Maybe you're right, but it was never for me. The AIA is *important*. You won't remember it, Miss Cortez, but the Director will. All of its agents do good, necessary work. The world is safer for their presence. Everything is changing, though. In your grandfather's time, Seattle alone had—"

"Like a dozen Inquisitors, yeah, I know. I wasn't there, but I can read. But I don't get what that has to do—"

"With more than a dozen on call. The regions shared resources. When I was first made liaison between the Inquisition and the bureaucracy, I had hundreds of people I could call for any emergency. Politicians, agencies, police commissioners, anything. Whatever it took to get the work done."

Mina looked to the Director, who nodded, with a frown. She gestured for Miss Lasko to continue.

"The world is no less dangerous than before. The bad guys are still out there, from the black market to human trafficking. The agency with the best record for dealing with them has been being nickeled and dimed to death year after year. Do you know much hemming and hawing there was over whether we should bring in a new agent when we were down to three?"

Deb—Deputy Mayor Lasko—was looking at her with passionate frustration, so Mina answered flatly. "Lots, I'm sure. Which is a perfectly reasonable explanation for killing people."

"You aren't getting it. We couldn't even bring in more civil servants to work around things. They wanted the whole thing forgotten.

Politicians talk about movement towards a less authoritarian state, that we're moving back towards the world as it was in some mythical golden age, and then following that up by making sure the AIA can't do its job effectively."

"So you started kidnapping people? Let the black market get hold of the agent-killer chips?" Mina started, angrily. "The Inquisition wasn't as awesome as it used to be, so you sabotaged it?"

"The chips were being managed. It was the black market being sabotaged. The cops and FBI agents had the only chips that weren't designed with catastrophic failure and rejection in mind. Very tragic for the crooks, I'm sure. I had it under control."

"Uh-huh," Mina said. "Sure. So you weren't trying to destroy the AIA?"

"I was trying to save the AIA! Once the emergency order was signed off on, things would have gone back to the way they're supposed to be. The chips would have been tracked down, the black market around Seattle—and plenty of other criminal enterprises—would be shut down cold, and there would be no question that four active agents hadn't been enough. A couple of extra chips being missing would have increased paranoia in other regions, seen their funding and recruiting pick back up."

Mina shook her head. "So you were playing the criminals and all those other agents?"

Miss Lasko shook her head. "The other agents were true believers. People I'd worked with, or people whose families, profiles, and history I knew well enough to be convinced that they'd see the necessity of a state of emergency to wake people up."

Mina shook her head. "How could they be that crazy? Their profiles—"

"Were of great benefit. It led me to just the right people."

"People like me?" she couldn't help but ask.

"Yes and no. You were a legend's granddaughter, who'd follow the leads put in front of her. Not the one we were looking for, but I hoped you'd do. We needed someone, particularly someone with your connection to the victims."

"Not the one you were looking for?"

"This wasn't supposed to happen yet, we weren't ready. You were supposed to be in Russia right now."

Mina caught on. She glanced at Miko a moment. "You were waiting for ..."

"For Miss Kimura, yes. High aptitude tests, rapid learning curve, physically fit, and absolutely no initiative. Same connection to the victims, and very little chance of defying orders. The same way she follows you around like a puppy now. Once you left, she'd be lost."

"Hey!" Miko started, pausing just as quickly. "Okay, so maybe."

Miss Lasko smirked. "No maybe about it. Plenty of vetting just to be sure. For one thing, I must have signed up for every committee even remotely related to your father." She looked back to the rest. "We just had to wait until Miss Kimura was of age to handle chipping. No one would blink at her getting an early chipping date. We'd have our agent, and everything was in place to ensure Mina was long since off to Russia."

Mina was taken aback, but as the words processed, had to admit some of it sounded right. Especially with Agent Park involved. She was pretty sure, between Miss Lasko and Agent Park stepping in as a mentor, Miko probably would have made more of the agent they were looking for. "So I was ..."

"An accident. We couldn't wait for Miss Kimura, and you fit the profile. Not perfectly, but we hoped to make it work. I'd already done my best to vet you in case worse came to worst, and having Tommy Escalante's granddaughter as a worst-case back-up didn't seem like a hardship at the time. I really did admire him."

"So, what happened to change the plan?"

"Your friend's boss got greedy. Not for money—that type of greed in a profile doesn't get his kind of job. When we were compromising University security anyway, he got greedy for information. He tried to use Raymond Harper's disruptions to build back doors into the school's systems. After all, if they were the ones doing the real chip programming, what else might be going on there? I'd worried he might get sloppy like that, but when this whole thing began, I was still trying to conserve assets. Get sloppy he did, though. So the emergency back-up it was. And as if that wasn't enough, then Agent Park had to be too smart for his own good."

Mina bristled.

Lasko continued, that sad look in her eyes all the more enraging in Mina's opinion. "We had to get Agent Hall more involved than we'd have liked. His partner noticed something was off and started poking around at the edges of our operation. I promise you, Miss Cortez, I regret having to have them killed. They were good men and good agents."

"Agent Park was, anyway," Mina agreed.

"You'll have an opportunity to ask any remaining questions later," The Director told her, getting some help from a young FBI agent to get around until she could get her arm rebooted. "For now, I'm going to join a full security team in taking her to secure holding. You should get some rest—you've earned it."

* * * *

Mina made sure she got to work a little early the next morning, even if she'd started out from a spare room at the FBI headquarters, while her apartment window was being repaired. She'd have to do the rest of the tidying herself. Of course, once she arrived, her parents were already there and working: her mother putting out arrangements in the refrigeration units, and her father double checking orders.

"Good morning, sweetie. Are you sure you're all right to be back so soon?" her mother asked, looking up as Mina came in.

"The doctors said so," Mina said, adding, "No riding my bike, no heavy lifting, regular breaks—I need to take it easy for a couple weeks, but I'm actually kind of looking forward to getting back to a bit of a routine."

"Good. We're behind," her father added.

"Really, honey, Mina has been through a lot. I mean, your daughter got shot. Are you positive you're ready, Mina?"

"I promise, Mom. Scott is back, the FBI caught the kidnappers, no one is after me. I'm just ready for everything to get back to normal for a little while." She meant it, too. She was pretty sure with the AIA, there would never be a proper normal, but she'd had enough excitement for a while.

"We can talk about it over breakfast," Mina's father responded, with a sigh. "We really are glad to have you back, but ... "

"I understand, I've been out for a while and everything is behind." Mina said, cutting off any further objection from her mother by fetching an apron and going to the back to start bringing some flowers forward to start putting together bouquets for display, and filling some of the arrangements. "Like I said, I've missed this place, especially when I wasn't sure I was going to see it again any time soon." Once again, it didn't take much for Mina to project absolute sincerity. She might be not telling them a lot, but she did miss the routine, after everything that had happened.

Despite her father's urgency and her mother's concern, they had breakfast together as a family, with very little discussion of flowers or landscaping. Instead, they wanted to know all of the details. Mina told them what she could, using the official cover story provided by the Director to fill in for some details. By and large, she was able to stick fairly close to the truth. A burglar had broken in, tied in with people who thought she might know something associated with Scott's kidnapping. She left out everything having to do with car chases, detective work, or the University. Her mother continued to express concern for some time thereafter, wanting to make sure that Mina was certain she felt all right, and was safe, and to make sure she knew she could come stay at the house again if she wanted to.

"That's okay, Mom, seriously. I kind of want to really focus on things getting back to normal for a while. That means finishing moving in and getting on with my new life."

"Miko will be by after her lessons, and will bring some more of your things from the house. Dr. Kimura even let her drop French for a little bit so she could have more time to help you out."

"As long as she doesn't drop aikido." Mina replied, with a small grin. Seeing her parents' blank expressions, she quickly added, "Miko really, really likes her aikido lessons. I know they're very important to her."

"Oh, well, all right then."

With questions answered, and Mina trying to express just how much she didn't want to relive the past few days more than necessary, which her mother seemed to eventually understand -- what was left was mostly work. Despite her previous impressions of impending doom due to an overload of flowers, Mina found herself getting back into the routine. She spent her breaks reviewing some of the current park proposals, despite her mother reminding her she didn't have to.

"I didn't think you cared much for the parks & rec projects?" her Father inquired, quizzically.

"Oh. Well, I kind of got to know one of the city liaisons on these a little bit. I'm kind of curious exactly what we're doing. Besides, eventually Scott is going to be doing more with his family's charity efforts and all, and I'd like to do my part."

"Well, there's a few projects I could use some help on, if you want to start taking on some supervisory work outside the shop too? Any preferences from the files?"

"Oh, um, while I was in protective custody, apparently something came up at the University. I guess there was a lot of damage. After all they did for me, I'd kind of like to help with the restoration as soon as it's budgeted."

"The University project? Sure, I'll pull up everything for that. Dr. Kimura will be helping a lot with any work there."

"I know, which is part of it, too, I admit," Mina replied. "Miko will be helping out, too."

"Amiko? I didn't think she had a lot of interest in landscape restorations."

"She doesn't, but it's something the Kimuras can do together. I got a chance to talk to them a little when he came to the FBI HQ last night. I guess she's going to do that, and he's going to start up cello lessons and pick aikido back up, so they have some things they can do together again."

"Well, then, I'm glad to hear it. Kind of like us all getting to work together here," he replied in good cheer.

Mina paused, a few different comments passing through her brain, before finally answering, "Yeah, kind of like that."

Miko showed up with Vlad, still dented and badly scratched up, but seemingly running fine. She came into the shop, helping out with the last few clean up details Mina needed to see to before the girls headed out. Mina took some extra time saying goodbyes for the day and waiting until both parents had their hands free to give each a hug before they left.

"Tired of flowers and ready to get back to car chases and spycraft yet?" Miko asked as soon as they were underway.

"Flowers are kind of appealing right now, actually. Maybe once I can walk without limping around. Besides, you know very well I can't tell you anything about any more cases, whether one is on or not."

"Pft, like you can hide anything from me. Besides, the Floral Avenger needs her trusty sidekick."

"My boss would be about ready to shoot me if she knew I was even humoring this conversation. I really, really don't like getting shot."

"Deny it all you will, that was kind of fun. Besides, she was already talking to me about clearances and maybe getting put in for consideration to join, or at least become a liaison in whatever I do."

"No. Getting shot was not fun," Mina answered with a smirk. "And second, joining anything won't be 'til at least next year when you get chipped. Until then, you're not supposed to be involved with anything for the AIA."

"Not the getting shot, duh. Seriously, at least admit the car chases were awesome."

"Depends. Can we drop this whole line of conversation?"

"Not a chance."

"All right, all right. Can we at least put it off' til later? Right now, I just want to get unpacked, put my kitchen back together, get some real food, and just be normal for a little—" He comm buzzed for her attention. Mina cringed, but checked it. "So, never mind. Can you drop me off somewhere I can get a lift to the University? I need to do some follow up at the labs real quick."

"Forget that. I have time, I'll take you myself."

Mina sighed. "I can't talk you out of this, can I?"

"I know the University better than you do, you'll get there much faster, and—"

"Okay, fine. Can we just get going then? They aren't expecting any big drama. It's just some following up, then we can go to the apartment and get to unpacking."

Miko wasn't listening, but adjusting her fedora and tipping her bobblehead's nose while they were stopped at a red light. "It's 106 miles to Chicago. We've got a full tank of gas, half a pack of cigarettes, it's dark, and we're wearing sunglasses." she said, looking to Mina expectantly.

"You don't smoke, and what does Chicago have to do with anything?"

"Hopeless. Totally hopeless."

About the Author

Jeffrey Cook lives in Maple Valley, Washington, with his wife and three large dogs. He was born in Boulder, Colorado and has lived all over the United States, but Washington has long since become home. He has been immersed in storytelling since very long car rides when he was six. *Mina Cortez: Bouquets to Bullets* is his fourth novel and first YA novel. He is the author of the *Dawn of Steam* series of alternate-history/early-Steampunk epistolary novels and has contributed to a number of role-playing game books for Deep7 Press out of Seattle. When not reading, researching, or writing, Jeffrey enjoys role-playing games and watching football.

jeffcook74@gmail.com
http://www.authorjeffreycook.com/
https://www.facebook.com/jeffrey.cook.54390
@jeffreycook74